Shut-Out!

Camilla Reghelini Rivers

James Lorimer & Company Ltd., Publishers
Toronto, 2000

James Lorimer & Company Ltd. acknowledges the support of the Ontario Arts Council. We acknowledge the support of the Government of Canada through the Book Publishing Industry Development Program (BPIDP) for our publishing activities. We acknowledge the support of the Canada Council for the Arts for our publishing program.

Cover illustration: Sharif Tarabay

Canadian Cataloguing in Publication Data

Rivers, Camilla Reghelini
    Shut-Out!

(Sports stories)
ISBN 1-55028-669-2 (bound)   ISBN 1-55028-667-6 (pbk.)

I. Title. II. Series: Sports stories (Toronto, Ont.).

PS8585.I8776S58 2000   jC813'.6   C00-930194-1
PZ7.R58Sh 2000

James Lorimer & Company Ltd., Distributed in the United States by:
Publishers   Orca Book Publishers
35 Britain Street   P.O. Box 468
Toronto, Ontario   Custer, WA USA
M5A 1R7   98240–0468

Printed and bound in Canada.

Contents

For all those who made this book possible:
My family; and Celine and Anthony Reghelini

1

No Place Like Home

David could hear them talking. They didn't know he was there. He hugged his knees, afraid to move. Dark eyes squeezed tight, he wished he was somewhere else. Anywhere, but in the front hall closet trying on his soccer cleats.

"A hundred dollars. Shirley, that's a lot, when money's tight," he heard Gramps say.

He could barely hear his mother over the kitchen clatter.

"For heaven's sake Dad, we're not that poor. I've always had enough for David's soccer registration."

"But to throw that kind of money away so an eleven-year-old can kick a ball around a field. I don't know ..."

"It's not throwing it away. David loves to play." His mom's voice had grown louder, harsher.

"Look, Shirley, you know I'd be the first to say 'Go ahead' if he was built like your brother Jake. But, face it, he's a runty kid — all skin and bones," Gramps said.

David sucked in his breath. The words had landed like a punch to his gut.

"Dad how could you? He's not a runt. He's just short. Anyway, the exercise is good for his asthma."

"Hey, if he needs exercise, let him walk to school. In my day —"

"Yeah, I know," his mother interrupted. "You walked three miles in rain and snow, froze your feet, yada, yada, yada. I've heard this all a hundred times. This is the city and things are different now."

"Okay, okay. Then get him to cut the lawn, shovel the walk. It wouldn't hurt him to help around the house."

"He does help, or haven't you noticed. David's playing soccer. End of subject." Cutlery rattled as a drawer slammed shut.

David let himself breathe again. He was going to play soccer. He should have felt happy, but he didn't. His insides were churning. Please don't let them start arguing again. He crossed his fingers. As if in answer to his prayer, he heard the scrape of a chair and Gramps' slippered feet in the hall.

For a while he listened to the sharp thud of his mother's knife on the cutting board. He knew she was upset. She always baked when she was unhappy.

"Got to get out of here without her knowing I heard," David muttered.

The storm in his stomach was getting worse. Suddenly the closet felt stuffy, filled with an overpowering smell of leather and his mom's perfume. Stale. I don't want to barf, he thought. To his relief, he heard his mother turn on a tap. He crawled out. Quickly. Quietly. The brass doorknob felt cool in his hand as he opened, then slammed the front door.

"Hi, Mom, I'm home," he called.

David gave his mother a big hug. She smiled with her lips, but her eyes were still sad. Trying to cheer her up he used the magic words, "I'm going to practice the organ now."

Scales. Pedals. Chords. Warmed up, he turned to *Skaters' Waltz*. David liked this song with its slow gliding melody. The knot in his belly loosened. He had learned this song especially for Gramps.

When he first heard that Gramps was moving in, he had danced around the house. "*All right* — Gramps, here whenever I need to talk. Wow."

"What? I'm not good enough?" His mother had stuck out her tongue, playfully.

"Oh, Mom, you know what I mean. Guy stuff."

"Guy stuff, huh? N*o-oo*, I guess I wouldn't do, would I?"

He'd wanted to do something big to celebrate. Awesome, he'd thought, as an idea had formed in his head.

"Take me to Treadwell's to get some music," he'd pestered his mother.

"I can't, David. I've got to get the spare room ready for Gramps."

"I promise I won't take long."

"*David.*"

"Please. I'll help with the room. Please, please ..."

Picking out the old fashioned songs, the ones he knew his grandfather would like, had taken longer than expected. This is great, he'd thought, as he'd assembled the perfect mix of fast and slow pieces.

His grandfather loved to hear him play. Every day he'd practiced hard. Mom had smiled a lot that week. Sometimes he'd heard her humming the tunes as she worked around the house.

The day Gramps moved in, his mother had cooked a wonderful dinner — golden roast potatoes, thick slices of beef and pie. The house had smelled so good — of cinnamon and apple.

Stuffed, they sprawled in the living room. Mom curled up on the sofa and Gramps sat in his favourite chair, an old plaid recliner. He had brought it with him. His worn, red slippers rested on the threadbare footrest. Everything looked so peaceful. So cozy. David reached over and stroked his grandfather's gnarled hand.

"I have a surprise for you," he said.

David played. Gramps and Mom kept time, or sang when they knew the words.

Then Gramps did something strange. In the middle of *There's No Place Like Home,* he suddenly got up and left.

"I'm not finished," David called after him.

Gramps didn't answer. He just went to his room.

"That's okay, David. Gramps is tired, dear. It's been a long day." His mother ruffled his thick black hair.

The next day the fighting had started.

* * *

The smell of hermits — his favourite cookie — wafted into the living room.

He turned off the organ and headed for the kitchen. On the table, in neat rows, his mother had laid the first batch to cool. He grabbed a couple.

"Don't eat too many. We're having spaghetti and meat-balls for supper," his mother warned.

"Shirley." Gramps shuffled into the room. "That boy's going to spoil his appetite if you let him gorge himself on sweets."

"Oh, Dad. For heaven's sake, it's only a couple of cookies. He's a growing boy. Want one?"

David didn't wait to hear the answer. He bolted outside.

It had been three long weeks since Gramps moved in, full of sharp words and unbearable silences. One thing for sure, Gramps had suddenly changed that night, and David didn't know why. His grandfather didn't want to do anything to-gether at all. What's more, every time he turned around, he ticked Gramps off.

David kicked the soccer ball against the garage door. Waited for the rebound, then kicked again. This living to-gether was the pits. Oh, how he missed the things he did with Gramps before the old man moved in. He kicked the ball harder. It hit the metal door with a loud crash.

There were no more walks in the park. *Crash*. No more playing chess. *Crash*. No more stories. *Crash*. And worst of all — no laughing or joking. *CRASH*.

Tears welled up in his eyes. He fought them back, putting his energy into another kick.

"Hey, Davie, better let me be goalie. That garage door needs protection."

David smiled. "Patrick, my man. Okay, show me what you're made of."

Patrick waddled up to the garage, stretched out his arms, and embraced the door. "I'm not going to let him hurt you any more, I promise."

David giggled. It felt good to laugh.

"Registered for soccer yet?"

"You bet. Went down to the club on the first day." Patrick shifted his chunky form into a crouch. "Come on Davie, try and get one past me."

"No problem, sieve." David kicked. The ball banged against the lower right hand corner of the garage.

"I let you have that one. Bet you can't do that twice."

David hoofed the ball again. Patrick lunged, his bulk displaying an unexpected agility.

"See I told you." He held the ball close to his chest.

"Yeah, right. Just a lucky save. Stop this one."

The ball and fake insults bounced between the boys. Laughter filled the air.

The door clicked open and David's mother's head peeked around it. "Patrick, your mother phoned. She wants you to head home."

"Oh man, I was just warming up. Thanks Mrs. DeMarco." He gave her a thumbs-up, then turned back to David. "Your shots are getting way better."

"You think so?" David bowed deeply. "And you, Oh Mighty Goalie, are as great as ever."

"Better believe it. I'm good." Patrick thumped his broad chest with his fists.

David watched his friend swing his pudgy frame onto his bike, then disappear around the corner. He couldn't help but smile. Patrick could make him laugh. Patrick didn't change. Patrick could be counted on.

"David. Supper," his mother called.

They sat eating, like a table of strangers. The only noise was the clatter of forks against plates.

When he was finished, Gramps rinsed his plate and left the room.

David picked up his mother's plate. He watched her as he scraped the half-eaten spaghetti into the garbage can. She rested her head on her bony arms. Limp, brown hair cascaded over the limbs and across the table when she put her head down.

Things had become so unsettled since his mother had lost her day surgery job. She had found another right away. But, what kind of job was this? The days and times were always changing. Sometimes she was gone before he left for school. Other times, she wasn't there when he got home.

"Shift changes go with the territory of being a ward nurse. At least I have a job. You'll get used to it."

It was two months now and he still wasn't used to it. He hated it.

David touched her lightly on the shoulder. "Mom, are you okay? I cleared the table."

"I'm fine, dear, just a little tired. Thanks." She lifted her head slightly and peered through the screen of mousy-brown hair.

Poor Mom, she was always tired now.

"What a mess!"

David jumped. He slowly turned to face his grandfather.

"Don't you know you're supposed to rinse the dishes and stack them beside the sink. You've made more work for your mom."

"But Gramps —"

"Don't you back chat, boy. Now take all those dishes out and rinse them. NO, not like that. Use hot water. Haven't you learned anything yet?"

David's mother took the plate, firmly, from his shaking hands. "Why don't you go do your homework?"

David fled from the room, relieved. He climbed the stairs two-by-two. He shut his bedroom door, leaned against it and let out a sigh. Homework? There wasn't any.

Absentmindedly, he picked up a marble and tossed it into the cup on his desk. Two points for Shaq — nothing but net. But that's basketball. He'd rather be playing soccer.

David tipped the cup over. With a flick of his finger, he sent the marble rolling into it. Bingo. He retrieved the marble and placed it in the middle of the desk. A quick jerk of the wrist sent the marble rolling from his right hand to his left.

"Number twelve — Shinkewski, passes to sixteen — Brock. A header to number eleven — DeMarco. WHAT A KICK."

The marble thunked into the cup. David leaned forward to get it.

"… want you to lay off of David," his mother's voice intruded into his haven.

"Now what did I do?" Gramps asked.

"You were yelling at him about the dishes."

"I wasn't yelling. I was just explaining to him that he did them wrong."

The constant bickering was getting to David. He put his hands over his ears. It didn't help. He could still hear the fight. He longed for the peace before Gramps moved in.

"... did as good a job as one can expect from a kid his age." His mom's voice was shaking.

"No point in doing a job, if you don't do it correctly in the first place, Shirley."

"He'll learn, Dad." Dishes banged on the table.

"Well, I was teaching him," Gramps said.

David grabbed his pillow and screamed into it. "STOP IT. Stop it, stop it ..." He turned on the radio to try and drown out the voices.

"... not your place to teach him." His mother's voice filtered through the music.

"Pardon me for trying to help. That kid needs a male role model. I've been it for the last eleven years. I'm not about to shirk my duty now."

"No one's asking you to. Just treat him a little gentler, that's all." There was a pleading tone to his mother's voice.

"I'll not be molly-coddling him like you do, Shirley. You'll turn him into a regular pantywaist."

Pantywaist? What's that, David wondered.

"Don't be ridiculous, Dad. David's not a sissy."

"Ridiculous? Me? Who's the one encouraging that soccer nonsense?"

Oh, great. Not that again. Why was Gramps so hung up on the soccer thing?

"There's nothing sissy about soccer," his mother said.

"Hrump," Gramps sniffed, ignoring her comment. "You're not doing him any favours by catering to him. Mark my words, he'll become as irresponsible as that father of his."

David gasped. Then held his breath — waiting. Waiting for what? He didn't know.

"Leave Vince out of this. Just leave him out," his mother yelled.

David's pent up tears started to flow, uncontrollably. Things were bad. They couldn't get much worse. He became

aware that his chest was tight. Breathing was becoming difficult. He fought to control his sobs. Would he be able to take
his inhaler while crying? His asthma was becoming a pain.
Stress could bring on an attack. And was he stressed now? You
bet!

With slow, deliberate moves he picked up the tiny canister, shook it, then expelled the air from his lungs. He brought
the mouthpiece to his lips. Plunging the top, he inhaled the
medication.

A door slammed downstairs. Silence. What a relief. Exhausted he fell onto the bed.

Things would be better tomorrow. Mom wouldn't be tired
tomorrow — it was her day off. And tomorrow soccer practice
started.

2

Pros Do Things Differently

"Patrick, my man. Give me five." David slapped his friend's meaty palm.

"Great day, Davie, great day."

It was a great day. The sun was shining. And it was warm. Unusual for April in Winnipeg. In the park, the pond was alive with ducks. Quacking filled the air. A light breeze carried the scent of crab apple blossoms. It ruffled the boys' hair as they made their way across to the soccer field.

In the centre, the new coach dribbled a ball between his feet. He tucked his toe under it and tossed the ball high into the air. Foot. Head. Shin. Knee. Any legal body part to keep the rally going. Soon there were fifteen pairs of eyes riveted on him. Jaws slackened with awe. The coach's pink face reddened. Sweat darkened his blond curls. He grabbed the ball and stopped.

"Sit ... down ... lads ..." Gulping air between each word, he tried to catch his breath. As he stood there panting, the boys whispered among themselves.

"Did you see that?" Adam's grey eyes were as big as saucers. He was the smallest kid on the team. Sandy, the class science-nerd, called him *Atom* because he always seemed to be in motion — even when sitting still.

"Five minutes straight. The ball never came near the ground. It defies the law of physics." Sandy said, scratching his blond head.

"Did you know that Ricardinho Neves juggled a regulation soccer ball for nineteen hours five minutes and thirty-one seconds in 1994," said Kevin, a human sports encyclopedia.

"Think he'll teach us how? Probably not." Rob folded his long arms, tucking his hands into his armpits. David felt sorry for him. He had become so pessimistic since his parents had split up last fall.

"Sure he will, and lots more. He played pro soccer in England, you know." Kevin blinked owlishly behind his thick lenses.

"Bet he was the team star. Like me." Myles thumped his muscular chest. He was so full of himself it made David gag.

"No kidding. Wonder if he's on a soccer card?" Stuart, the resident card collector, asked.

"Naw. He didn't play for long. Got hurt. Did permanent damage, my dad said so." In Kevin's mind his dad was as valid a source as any record book.

"Yeah ... well he still could be. Nerds like your dad don't know squat. Bet he's on a rookie card." Myles glared at Kevin, daring him to disagree.

"Hey ... wouldn't that be neat. Want to go to *Sports Card Connection* after practice, to check it out?" Jon pulled another candy out of his pocket from his seemingly endless supply and popped it into his mouth.

"Count me in," a number of the boys answered together.

Patrick nudged David. "I'm going, are you?"

"I'd like to, but I doubt it, music lesson night."

The coach cleared his throat to get the boys' attention.

"I'm Colin Prescott. Your coach for the season. You can call me Coach Prescott. Has a nice ring to it, don't you think?" He gave a little laugh, then he cleared his throat again.

"Anyway ... soccer is a great sport, but I'm sure you know this already, lads, or else you wouldn't be here. It's a game of skill. A thinking man's game. A game ..."

David's mind started to wander as the coach droned on. He snapped himself back to earth and tried to pay attention.

"... team works as a single unit to achieve a common goal. It's my job to make you into that unit. I'll work hard to teach you. But you must work hard, too. You put your minds to it, dedicate yourselves. Great things will happen."

Patrick poked David in the ribs.

"First time coach," he whispered.

"How can you tell?"

"Talks too much. Majorly nervous, I guess."

"Okay, lads. Firstly, I want to divide you into two groups," the coach said.

"Trade places with Sandy. Quick." David jabbed Patrick with his elbow.

"What for?"

"You do want to be on the same team, don't you? That way we'll both be two's when he numbers us."

"Good thinking."

But Prescott didn't number the team. He picked up two orange pylons and headed across the field instead.

"Form two parallel lines, lads," he called back at them. "You're going to race to see which team you're on."

David looked across at his partner. His heart dropped. Myles — tall, muscular, all-round athlete. He looked at Patrick and slashed his own throat with his finger.

Patrick laughed. "No kidding. Going to need a rocket to keep up with that one, Davie."

"Might as well give up now, twerp. No point in embarrassing yourself." Myles smirked at David and flexed his muscles.

Coach Prescott rubbed his hands together. "Okay, lads. Let's have a go."

As each pair made their way across the finish line, Prescott took down their names on a piece of paper. He directed the winner of the race to his right and loser to the left. David kept a close eye on the losers. He knew he'd be joining them.

"Ouch! What did you do that for, you dork?" David's cheek stung. He dusted off what was left of the clump of hardened mud Myles had chucked.

"Hey, pay attention then. We're up next, stupid," the other boy replied.

David was seething. I'll show that meathead, he thought.

When the coach blew the whistle he took off like the wind. But in two steps Myles was ahead of him. David pumped his legs harder. The gap between them narrowed. He tapped into a reserve he didn't know he had, and almost caught up to the bigger boy. But not quite. He watched as Myles kept running, straight to the winning group — making the coach walk over to him to get his name.

"Hey, sucker. I told you I'd leave you in the dust," the bigger boy called to David.

"As if," he replied.

Patrick touched his shoulder. "I thought you were toast. But, you sure fooled us all."

"You bet. I was only three steps behind him."

"Yeah ... Right."

"Okay, okay. Five steps. Anyway, it was close."

"Too bad close only counts in horseshoes — you still ended up with the losers."

"Yeah, well so did you." David shoved Patrick playfully.

"Ain't that the truth. No partner. No race."

"Uneven numbers, I guess."

"Listen up, lads. I want the group on my left to get a partner," the coach said.

David pointed at Patrick. "You and me, okay?"

He nodded yes.

"The drill you will be doing goes like this," Prescott continued his instructions. "Dribble a couple of metres. Pass the ball to your partner. He dribbles for a bit and passes it back to you. And so on. By the end of the season you lads will be able to get rid of the ball quickly and accurately. Now off you go. Down to the far end of the field."

The boys did as they were told. Putting everything into the drill. But after half an hour the practice started to drag.

"This is bo-ring," Rob flicked a lock of chestnut hair off his forehead.

"When's he going to come and give us another drill?" David asked.

"Good question." Patrick pointed to the other group taking shots on goal. "They're not just dribbling the ball down there."

"Now, that looks like fun." David passed the ball.

"Look who's in goal."

"That's Sandy *Captain Kirk* McDonald! Poor kid."

"No kidding. He standing there like a pylon. First Prescott makes him change groups and now that. It takes a special kind of person to be a goalie." Patrick passed the ball back.

"Yeah. A sucker for punishment. Like you." David dribbled the ball then kicked it.

"Ha, ha." His friend booted the ball back. Hard.

They started to make a game of who could hoof the ball at the other the hardest.

The coach still didn't come. But it didn't matter — David was having fun. It was great to be playing soccer again.

Finally Prescott waved them in. The practice was over.

They walked to the parking lot with Sandy.

"We saw what Prescott did to you, man. Put you in goal. That must have sucked," David said.

"Affirmative. But resistance is futile. I will be assimilated. The coach says I have the right build for the position. He says he'll help me. I'm to be team goalie." Sandy looked up to the sky and laughed. "Beam me up, Scottie, and put me out of my misery."

"If you don't like it, why did you sign up?" David asked.

"Space camp."

"Huh?"

"My father said, if I sign up for a sport each year, I can go to Space Camp when I'm fourteen. For that, I can put up with anything."

"Yeah, but why soccer? You could have done tennis or something," Patrick said.

"Logic. Pure logic. Large numbers — my cloaking device. With twenty-two players on the field, no one will notice *the one*. And that's me." He pointed at his chest with both thumbs. "Anyway it's not so bad, I guess."

"Hey, Space Cadet, get your butt in here. We got important things to do," Myles yelled.

"Got to go. My shuttle awaits — car-pooling with Myles." He gave the *live long and prosper* sign.

"Well, I don't think it's working. The invisibility thing," David laughed.

"No kidding. And what's worse, he has to car pool with the jock. His father sure knows how to torture him. See you."

David yanked open his mom's car door. "Some of the guys are going to check if they made a collector card of Coach Prescott. He played pro soccer. Can I go?"

His mom shook her head. "I'm sorry, David, you know you can't. You haven't had supper yet. Music lessons — or have you forgotten? Maybe next time."

"Just thought I'd ask." David smiled as he crawled into the passenger seat.

"So … how did it go?" His mother put the car into gear and they started to move.

"Mom, it was wicked. Coach Prescott is awesome. You should see what he can do with a ball. And he's so friendly — calling us lad or Jocko. Neat, huh? Boy, did James look dorky when the coach called him Jocko — he was clueless."

David's eyes were big and shining. His hands were moving as if they had a life of their own. He hadn't even stopped to take a breath as he spoke. His mother couldn't help herself — she burst out laughing.

"That good, huh?" she asked.

"Oh, Mom, even better. I almost tied Myles in a race. I was awesome."

"Myles? The fastest boy in the class, Myles?"

David nodded. "Yup. The one who'll pound it into you so you won't forget."

"Wow."

"You'll never guess who's playing this year — *Captain Kirk*." He gave his mother the *live long and prosper* sign.

"You're kidding? Sandy McDonald — the *Trekkie*? Whatever possessed him?"

"Well, his dad said if he'll play a sport he can go to Space Camp. Anyway, what I wanted to tell you was, Coach Prescott is good. He's got Sandy trying out for goalie, and not hating it. Can you imagine that?"

"Neat trick. How'd he do that?" His mother pulled into the driveway. She turned off the motor and swiveled to face David.

"I don't know. But he got Sandy to go in goal for this shooting drill."

"Well, was he any good?"

"Heck no." David shook his head vigorously. "But he thinks he's going to be team goalie — *as if*. Claims the coach said he had a great build for the position."

"I'm sure the coach was trying to boost his confidence," she said.

"Yeah. Maybe."

"Gosh. Look at the time. Quick. You've only got fifteen minutes to eat before we leave for music. Hey, you're forgetting your inhaler."

David reached back into the car and grabbed the fanny-pack that held his medication.

"So how was your breathing?" she called as she rushed into the kitchen.

He dropped his things by the door and headed after her. "Fine. Didn't need to use it again."

"Great stuff." She filled a bowl with chili.

David could see the concern in her eyes. She worried too much. After all, the doctor had said he was only mildly asthmatic. But she made him take his inhaler faithfully before he exercised. He wrinkled his nose as he poured himself a glass of milk and sat down to eat.

"Aren't you and Gramps eating?"

"We finished earlier — seems we're grabbing a bite on the run more and more often."

Tell me about it, he thought. Supper had been a time to relax and tell Mom about his day. He had liked meal times, at least until Mom got her new job and Gramps moved in. Now meals were rushed, with Mom dashing off to work, or silent — each of them lost in their own thoughts.

* * *

David broke the silence.

"Well? Was there a card?"

"Huh ...? What ...?" Patrick kept staring into his bottle of Gatorade.

He had come over after David's music lesson to talk. But he hadn't done much talking.

"Collector card? Soccer card — of Coach Prescott? You did go with the others to check didn't you?"

"Yeah."

David dipped his finger into his Coke and flicked it at Patrick.

"Hey." His friend looked up for a moment.

"Well, Patrick, was there?" He reached over and lightly backhanded the boy's arm.

"Oh ... no. Guess he wasn't good enough, or famous enough, whatever. Come on, let's take these drinks outside okay?"

The door closed behind them before Patrick spoke again.

"What do you think of the coach?"

David zipped up his jacket. He leaned against the garage wall and let the warm stone heat his back. The evenings sure cooled down fast, he thought.

"He's awesome. I still can't believe what he did with that ball," David said.

"No, that's not what I mean. I mean what do you think of his coaching."

"Okay, I guess. You really couldn't tell from today."

"Exactly. You've got to admit something's screwy." Patrick took another swig of his Gatorade.

"You're joking, right?"

"No, something's weird. I'm not sure what." Patrick's forehead was creased in a frown.

"Patrick, you're sounding paranoid. Been reading too many *Hardy Boys* books?"

"No seriously, Davie, look at how he divided us into groups. Winners and losers. What kind of system is that?"

"Are you crazy? It sure beats going one-two, one-two, around the team. Patrick, it was only a race. It was fun."

"Whatever. But not having a partner should have made me an automatic winner."

"Or loser. It depends on how you look at it. So what? You should be happy. We're in the same group."

"Oh ... I'm happy, but —"

"Look, Patrick, he's a pro. He's British. He does things different. He must know more. See what he's doing for Sandy."

"That's another thing. Kevin won his race fair and square, and Sandy lost his, so why did Prescott switch them? You tell me that, huh?"

"Well ... didn't he say something about Sandy being a strapping lad?"

"Yeah, Davie. That idiot coach also said Sandy had an off race. Heck, I can beat him with my legs tied together."

"No kidding. Sandy sure can fool you, the way he's built and all. He hates sports."

"Looks like a racehorse. Too bad he moves like a drunken donkey." The boy danced a hopping-tripping step.

David rolled in the grass laughing. "Patrick. Stop. My stomach hurts."

His friend flopped down beside him.

"You're bad, Patrick. I like Sandy. He knows all kinds of neat stuff."

"Well, you wouldn't have today. When we were at the card shop, Myles and his friends were calling Kevin and me rejects. Sandy was in there, like, big time."

"Maybe all that attention from the coach has gone to his head."

"If that's what Prescott's attention does for Sandy, he can keep it. Maybe the coach should have given us some of it. He ignored our group the whole practice."

"I don't think he was ignoring us. You heard what he said, 'By the end of this season, you will be able to get rid of the ball quickly and accurately,' " David mimicked the coach.

"Davie, face it, he set us up dribbling and then he left." Patrick punched his left hand with his right fist for emphasis.

"I think the coach likes to work with small groups — just like Miss Ross does in math class."

"But Miss Ross comes and works with each group. He didn't."

"Just wait. He will. Next time will be our turn, you'll see."

* * *

But it wasn't. Not the time after that, either. Each practice was the same — the coach would set them dribbling and then go off and work with the other group.

He was starting to give up hope by the third practice. And then ...

"IT'S OUR TURN."

"Our turn? In your dreams, Davie."

"No, Patrick, look —"

"NO, *you* look. Practice with Prescott means dribbling this stupid ball, up and down this stupid field, while he plays at coaching down there." Patrick pointed over his shoulders with his thumb.

David grabbed his friend and turned him to face where the other group was. "See."

At that end they were doing a passing drill, too. The coach and Sandy, on the other hand, were bumping and pushing their way across the field. Each struggling to retain possession of the ball.

Patrick grabbed his chest and staggered.

"Oooh, my heart. My heart. The king is coming. The king is coming. And look, he's bringing his court jester, too. I can't take this shock. I'm having a heart attack." He fell on the grass twitching.

The other boys quickly rewarded him with laughter.

David reached down and pulled Patrick to his feet. "Shush, they'll hear you."

"So? Why should I care? He doesn't care about us."

"That's not true. He's ... he's ... our coach." David knew his voice betrayed his doubts.

But the coach was coming and his wobbling trust in adults steadied for a moment.

"Lads, we have some important work to do." Coach Prescott was beaming at them.

This was more like it. The air whooshed out of David's lungs. He hadn't realized he was holding his breath.

"We're going to do a one-on-one. No defence. Just you against the goalie. Let's take it from about fifteen metres out and straight down the middle. Okay, boys, hustle and give it your best shot. Sandy, are you ready, lad?" Coach Prescott tousled the boy's blond hair.

"Affirmative, I guess, but I suck."

"Nonsense. You'll do just fine. Okay, let's give it a go, lads."

"With *Da spas* in the goal, we're going to look great." Kevin pushed his glasses up his nose with his index finger. "Let's show the coach what we can do. My dad says, 'In sports, actions speak louder than words.'"

As each boy ran down the field and shot, there were cheers.

"All-*right*."

"Nice one."

"Way to go."

"Eight up — eight goals. OKAY."

"See, coach. I warned you. You cannot defy the laws of physics. I'm just no good," Sandy said.

"Rubbish. You just need a little coaching, Jocko." Prescott waved to the shooters to try once more.

"Let's do it again. Eight in the goal," Patrick said.

"Think we can? I don't know ..." Rob shook his head doubtfully.

David carefully maneuvered the ball down the field. He could see Coach Prescott's lips moving, so he strained to listen.

"... easy lad, take your time. That's it. Wait ... wait ..."

This is crazy. I'm in too close. I should have shot already he thought. But he followed instructions.

"Okay, lad, make your move ... NOW."

David kicked, trying for a corner of the goal. But he was off stride. Sandy scooped up the ball.

"Whooping warp drive, I saved it. Coach. I saved it." His hazel eyes opened wide. He was stunned.

"I knew you could, lad. I knew you could."

Disappointed, David returned up the field.

"What were you doing? Your timing was way off, Davie." Patrick shook his head.

"I know. Rob must have jinxed me. I was just following instructions."

"What instructions? The coach said give it your best shot and that wasn't it."

"Coach Prescott was calling instructions. Didn't you hear him?"

"Davie. Oh, Davie. Those weren't for you. They were for Sandy."

"Oh." David felt his face flush red. He had been so sure they were meant for him.

"Hey, don't sweat it. We all make mistakes. Oops, my turn."

David focused his attention on Coach Prescott. If he listened carefully, he could just make out what the man was saying. Sandy was getting a steady patter from the coach. And Sandy's confidence grew.

"Okay, lad, don't try to second guess the forward. Look him straight in the eye — he'll give himself away. Don't come so far out of the goal. Let them come to you. Good work, lad."

Throughout the practice, Prescott focused on Sandy. He only interacted with the other boys when he needed them to demonstrate something.

"That should be me. I've played goalie since I was five. It's not fair." Patrick punched his fist into the palm of his left hand.

"Don't worry, Patrick, you'll get your chance once Coach Prescott sees how good you are. You got us to the championships last year, didn't you?" David put his arm around his friend's shoulder.

"Oh, man."

Sandy had stopped another shot.

"Beam me up, Scotty. Straight to heaven." The coach high-fived Sandy's *live long and prosper* sign.

"Hey, he robbed me." Kevin shook his head in disbelief.

"Told you our luck wouldn't hold. *Captain Kirk* McDonald ain't no spastic anymore. He's getting the hang of things." Rob sighed.

"He should be. Look at all the coaching he's getting," Patrick snapped back.

3

Ghosts in the Game

"Sell the house? My wedding gift to your mother? I won't do it, Shirley. What's wrong with you? Did your heart turn to stone once you hooked up with that man?" The anger in Gramps' voice stopped David in his tracks. But it was his mom's words that turned him to stone. She spat them out in a hoarse whisper.

"That man, Dad? That man? You couldn't call him 'Vincent' or 'Vince' or 'your husband' or even 'David's father.' Oh, no. With you it's always 'that man.' You'd think he was a monster."

"Dad," David murmured. "Dad." Savouring the feel of the word on his tongue and palate. A feeling of longing came over him.

David changed his mind about going into the house. He sank down onto the back stairs. Thank goodness spring had come early. At least he wouldn't freeze staying away from the fighting.

"If the shoe fits," Gramps spat back. "Look how he left you to raise the kid alone."

"For heaven's sake. You act like he abandoned David and me. Can't you get it through your thick skull? He died, Dad. He died …" His mom's voice quivered as she spoke.

David tried to swallow the lump in his throat. *Dad* — the name he had never called anyone.

"And whose fault was that? If he'd only had enough sense to stay at home. Where he belonged. No. Instead, off he went to play a stupid soccer game." Gramps' voice had lost some of its volume but none of its edge.

David dropped his head in his hands. He had heard only good things about his father from his mother. And Gramps? Well, he never spoke about him at all. Now Gramps was talking and David wasn't sure he wanted to hear. But something held him there, forcing him to listen.

"It wasn't just a game. It was a tournament. He couldn't let his teammates down," his mother said.

You tell him, Mom. David knew what it meant to be a part of a team.

"But, you were expecting. He had responsibilities."

"You can't stop living just because your wife is having a baby," his mom said. Calmer. Firmer. "Anyway ... he could have stayed in Brandon for the weekend, like the other guys."

"Maybe he should have. Driving tired showed poor judgement. No wonder he smashed up his car." Gramps raised his voice again.

"Lord, Dad, sometimes I'd like to shake you. You know the accident wasn't his fault. The police said so. The truck was on the wrong side of the road. The driver was drunk. You can't blame everything on Vince." Her soft-spoken words were steady and strong.

"Doesn't matter. He should have stayed home. He spent far too much time playing soccer."

David gave his head a shake. There was Gramps on that soccer thing again — give it a rest already.

"Soccer got him killed. Irresponsible, that's what he was. And when you were with him, it rubbed off on you," Gramps continued.

"That's not true. He had a job *and* was taking classes at university. I was a full-time nursing student."

Irresponsible. David tried to imagine his mother doing something stupid. He couldn't. She was the most dependable person he knew.

"Oh, come on now. Look how you jumped into marriage, before you finished your nurse's training. A year later there was an unplanned baby on the way. Would it have hurt you to have waited two measly years?"

That baby they're talking about is me, David thought. Didn't they want me?

"I don't regret anything I did. Not for a moment. As it turned out, Vince and I only had a short time together. If we had waited there wouldn't have been a David. That alone makes everything worthwhile." His mother's words — gentle, loving — made him want to run in and hug her. But he didn't. Relieved, he sat there taking deep breaths.

"I don't know what you're complaining about. I kept up my schoolwork. I got my degree," she continued.

"Thanks to your mother and me. You never gave that a thought, did you? At her age, she should have been enjoying her golden years. Traveling. Not looking after a baby. It was hard on her," his grandfather said.

The guilt was back. An image flashed through his mind of Grammie, old and tired, rocking a wailing baby as she tried to bake cookies. *Strange,* a part of his mind noted, while another part cried, "Why does everything always point back to me?"

"Now you're barking up the wrong tree. Mama was a homebody. You liked to travel. Anyway, I tried to put him in daycare, but she would have none of it," his mother said of Grammie.

Gramps brushed off her words with a gruff mumble. "He was her first grandchild. What did you expect her to do?"

"She loved every minute of it. Dad, admit it. David was the apple of her eye and she was his."

"Okay, okay," Gramps said grudgingly.

There was silence. Silence, punctuated by the sound of a spoon clinking in a cup.

"Boy, were they close. From the moment he could crawl, he followed her around like an adoring puppy," his mom broke the quiet.

"Yeah ..." Gramps' tone had softened. "He liked to copy everything she did. I can still see him waddling after your mother, 'hepping Grammie dust,' he'd say. Using that tattered blue blanket of his. Leaving fingerprints or drool on her newly polished furniture. She never said boo, though."

"Remember the time she had just spent hours planting all those flowers?"

This is better, David thought. He leaned back on his elbows.

"Gosh — she let out one heck of a screech. I thought something awful had happened," Gramps added.

"Me, too. But by the time I got there, she was laughing so hard tears were flowing down her cheek," his mom said.

"And there was the little munchkin, beaming." Gramps chuckled.

"Covered in mud." Mom started to giggle.

"Offering this enormous bouquet of flowers to Grammie. He had plucked every gol-darn plant that had a blossom." His grandfather cut in.

"Roots and all. I was so upset. 'Don't you scold him, Shirley,' she told me. She just accepted David's bouquet. Arranged them in a vase. Then she went out and bought some more."

"She was some lady." Gramps sighed.

"Yeah ..." his mom murmured.

They lapsed into silence again. The squabble seemed forgotten. At least they still agreed on something.

He opened the front door. Quietly, he tiptoed up to his room. He didn't want them to hear him. He didn't want to spoil the truce.

Ghosts, David thought. Ghosts. That whole argument had been about two people who were dead. Long dead.

He tried to remember Grammie, but could think of nothing. At least nothing clear. Only fragments. Were they memories? He wasn't sure. Maybe they were pictures he had created from photographs and other people's recollections. The brain could do funny things.

All his life he had heard how close he had been to his grandmother. She had died when he was three. But try as he might, he couldn't remember any special memories. Smells, now they were a different thing. If he smelled moist rich black dirt or furniture polish — the old-fashioned kind, not the new lemon stuff — the name Grammie would come unbidden to his mind. He'd get a warm, happy feeling all over.

There was also the memory of the taste of the best chocolate chip cookies in the world. He couldn't remember actually eating one. But no chocolate chip cookie he tasted could measure up to the memory. Sometimes the crunch was wrong, or the flavour, or the texture. So, his mind would echo with "Not like Grammie's."

David sighed. He didn't even try to remember his father. He had died before David was born.

Reaching under his bed, David pulled out a large green plastic bin — his treasure box. It contained all the odds and ends that were dear to him. He pushed aside a couple of his favourite T-shirts that he had outgrown. He removed a plush rabbit and gently laid it on the bed. One eye was missing and the fur was matted. It was the only gift that he had ever received from his father — bought for him before he was even born. There, under it, was a package. The ten-inch by twelve-inch rectangle was wrapped in what looked like a gray rag. As David carefully unwrapped the package, it became clear that the cloth was a blanket. At one time it had been blue. Safely encased in the fabric was a white satin photo album trimmed in ivory lace. Across the cover, embroidered in silver thread, were the words *Memories for David*. Grammie had made it for him, or so his mom had told him.

He opened the first page. His own dark eyes stared back at him. The face, though, was of a man in his mid-twenties. Loose black curls framed the smiling face. David reached up and touched his own hair, as dark as the man's in the picture, but straight. Would he look like this when he grew up? Not likely. This man looked like he didn't have a care in the world. His eyes twinkled as if he was about to pull a fast one on you.

David flipped through the first few pages. There were about twenty pictures, all with his father in them. Here was one of him graduating from high school. There was one of his parents' wedding. Another one was with a group of men and women. His mom was in this one, too. Nona and Poppa DeMarco, David's other grandparents, were standing beside his parents. Under the photo was written "Mom and Dad on our honeymoon in Italy." And there was his favourite photograph — the one of his father lying on the sofa hugging Hop-a-long. It was the same rabbit now missing an eye and relegated to his treasure trunk. Sprinkled among these pictures were snap shots of his dad playing soccer.

All the photos had one thing in common. His father was happy — laughing, joking. How could anyone not like this man? But Gramps obviously didn't.

The truce didn't last long. By the evening they were scrapping again. The week that followed was filled with silent tension broken by sporadic fights. So when David saw his uncle's car pull up, he was hopeful for a change in mood, maybe even a laugh or two. Uncle Jake was a joker.

"Where's your mother? In the kitchen?" Uncle Jake pushed past David.

He was wrong. There was no "Hi, Sport" or "How's it going kid?" David felt cheated. His uncle had always made time for him. Dragging his feet, David followed Jake.

As he passed the organ, he caught sight of the reflection of his mom and her brother. Their fractured images were trapped in the glass of the French doors that separated the living room from the kitchen. He hesitated, then sat down on the organ bench and pretended to practice. He wanted to hear what they were saying. Eavesdropping was becoming a habit.

He glued his eyes to the doors watching their pantomime. As good as TV, he thought. Uncle Jake looked like Gramps. Why hadn't he noticed it before? Maybe it was because his uncle's stocky body was just starting to become paunchy. His brown hair was thinning, — just where the older man's bald spot was. But it was the lines around his eyes and mouth that clinched it. They had deepened and were now mirroring his grandfather's wrinkles.

"Look, Shirley, you and the old man had better get your acts together. I don't have the time to run over and stop petty squabbles." Jake even sounded like Gramps. David had never seen him upset before.

"This isn't a petty squabble. It's important. He refuses to even think about selling the house. I didn't tell Dad, but I've had to have the house boarded up. Someone went on a window smashing spree."

Gramps was going to hit the roof when he found out. He loved that house.

"Oh, great. Why did you make him move out and leave the building vacant? You were just asking for trouble."

"Jake, wake up. That place takes a lot of work. Dad can't do it any more. And now that I work shifts, I can't run between two houses. I just don't have the time. If you want to do the work you're more than wel —"

"Homecare. How about homecare?" his uncle interrupted.

"Don't you think I looked into it? He's a stubborn old mule. 'Won't have strangers pawing through my stuff,' he told me."

Yup, that's Gramps all right. There were some things of Grammie's even David was not allowed to touch. Come to think of it, most everything was off limits to him except her piano. That he was encouraged to play. His grandfather said it felt like Grammie was in the room when David made music.

"Then why didn't you and the kid just move in with him? Would have saved a lot of hassle," Uncle Jake said.

No way, man. David wasn't moving anywhere. He wasn't leaving his home. He wasn't leaving his neighbourhood. And he sure as heck wasn't leaving Patrick.

"Tried that already. Remember? When Vince died. Those two years were an eternity. I felt like I had never left home. Same room. Same routine. And what was worse, he treated me like a kid. It was, 'Where're you going?' 'Take a jacket.' 'When will you be back?' No thanks. I don't want to go through that again."

Way to go, Mom. Relief. Then guilt. Poor Gramps. He had to leave his home, his friends. No wonder he wasn't happy.

"Oh cripes, Shirley. I hope you didn't tell him that, did you?"

"Of course not. Give me some credit. I showed him the money we'd save. I told him we could help each other."

"Don't kid yourself, Sis. He'd never have left the house just for a few bucks. He'd have insisted you move in with him. End of subject."

"Oh, don't think he didn't try but, I had an ace in the hole. I told him that David was settled and happy here. It wouldn't be good to move him in the middle of the school year, now would it? See? I hit him where it hurt. You know he would do anything for David — well, almost anything." His mom was smiling like the Cheshire Cat.

David sat stunned. Oh, Mom. Oh, Mom how could you? That's why Gramps is mad at me. It's my fault he had to leave his home.

"Why you conniving little sneak. I didn't know you had it in you." Uncle Jake rubbed his hands together.

"Stop it." His mother swatted his uncle lightly on the arm. "Will you help me, please?"

"Aw, Sis ... What do you want me to do?"

"Talk to him."

"You're kidding? Me?" Jake started to laugh, then stopped.

"You're serious, aren't you? When would he ever listen to anything I've got to say?"

"He'll listen to you. He really will. He admires you. He's always holding you up as a role model for David." Mom reached over and patted Jake's hand.

No kidding. Gramps often said, 'Hard work is the key to success. Look at your Uncle Jake — started out tinkering with cars, now he owns his own business. You won't go wrong if you follow his example.' How could his uncle not know that Gramps was proud of him?

"Well, I'll be ... He's never said anything positive about me since I refused to go to college."

"You know how he is — too stubborn to admit he was wrong. But he does respect you. Will you talk to him?"

"Oh, all right. I'll try, but, I'll do it my way and in my own time. Agreed?"

David's mother nodded in reply.

"So where's the old coot now?"

"The park. Stormed out. Just because I brought up selling the house again. Gosh, Jake, we have been fighting all week. Can you believe we even had a fight about Vince? He's been dead for over eleven years, for heaven's sake."

"Dad sure had it in for him."

"Tell me about it. Dad couldn't forgive Vince for spoiling the plans that he had laid out for me. University, graduation, marriage — in that order." Mom's finger tapped the table for emphasis.

"Well?"

David jumped. He hadn't heard his grandfather walk in.

"She's called in the cavalry has she?" He strode into the kitchen.

"Oh. You're back?" His mom raked at her hair nervously.

"Hi, Dad. Just dropped in for a cuppa'." Uncle Jake pushed a chair out from the table with his foot. "Here take a load off. Wouldn't mind another cup, Shirley."

His mother took the mug he handed her and refilled it. She also poured one for Gramps.

"Checked the stock market lately? Business is booming. Remember Ted? The builder? He says he can't make houses fast enough. Pity people looking for homes. It's a seller's market, I tell you. A seller's market. I envy anyone with a house for sale. Anyway … How about those Blue Jays?" His uncle started in on his favourite topic.

David drifted out of the living room. When Gramps and Jake talked about baseball it was just dead boring — all stats and such. He didn't understand any of it.

4

Hornets' Sting

David admired himself in the bathroom mirror. He was ready to dart like a dragonfly and sting like a bee. Or in this case, a hornet. He smiled at his joke.

The HORNETS sounded good and fast. His hand brushed down the front of his black and gold shirt. Number 11. It was his lucky number, at least for this year. Each year he tried to get the sweater number to match his age. When he started playing soccer, the coach had handed him sweater number 5. He had been five years old at the time. It was just a coincidence. But it had been a good year, so David had made the number thing his personal sports superstition. So far it had worked for him.

This year he didn't have to scramble for number 11. Nobody wanted it. The shirt had been tossed out of the box and lay in the grass. It had a hole under one arm and one of the numbers was hanging by a few threads. Mom had fixed it to look as good as new.

The shorts were another matter. There hadn't been a pair small enough. David lifted the shirt to see them. The stupid things looked like a black skirt. He pulled at the waist where his mom had made two uncomfortable tucks. At least they wouldn't fall off. He let the shirt drop. Thank goodness it was long enough, even when tucked in, to hide the ugly waistband of the shorts.

He gave himself the once-over, then headed for the stairs.

"Why don't you come with us, Dad?" His mother's voice floated up.

"Got better things to do," Gramps replied.

"It's a beautiful day. You'll be sorry you missed it."

"I have no intentions of missing this lovely spring evening. I'm going to the park to feed the ducks," Gramps said.

"Oh, Dad. You can do that any day. Please come. It's his first game this season. You'd make him so happy."

"Shirley, lay off of me. I told you I'm not going. I don't want to watch a bunch of kids make fools of themselves."

"DAD — oh great."

David walked into the kitchen in time to see the back door close behind Gramps.

His mother turned. "Ah, there you are. Ready to go, dear?"

He wanted to erase the frown from her forehead. He wanted to say, it doesn't matter, Mom. I don't care if Gramps comes or not. But he couldn't. It did matter. So he squeezed her hand in reply.

The pre-game bustle erased Gramps from his mind. David listened intently to the coach's pep talk, focusing on the task at hand.

He had hoped to be on the starting line-up but wasn't surprised when he was not. There were three other boys sitting on the sidelines with him, all from his practice group. Each time the whistle blew, they retied their shoelaces, pulled up their socks and stood up expectantly. But each time play resumed without them, so, they sat down again — all except David. He couldn't sit still. He flitted along the sidelines — a black and yellow hornet — following the play.

The whistle blew for the fifth time. David was puzzled. Coach Prescott still wasn't calling for subs. The other team had changed players twice already.

"Still think Prescott's going to give everyone a chance, sucker?" Patrick's meaty fist landed a gentle punch on David's shoulder.

"He's got to. This is the house league. I read the handout they gave when I registered."

"So did I Davie, so did I. But did Prescott?"

"I wouldn't be surprised if we didn't get to play," said Rob as he pulled out handfuls of grass and tossed it.

"Why would you say that?" David's eyes widened. That horror was unthinkable.

"Well ... Look who's sitting out. We're all part of the Rejects." Kevin ran his hand through his wavy hair.

"The what?" David shook his head.

"The Rejects. That's what Myles and Sandy have been calling our practice group." Kevin squinted up at David through his thick lenses.

"Davie, you're so dumb. Look at us. We look like rejects." Patrick put his arm around David's shoulder, protectively. "You don't get it, do you?"

"I'm not a reject and neither are you." David shrugged off his friend's arm.

"I didn't say we were. I said we *looked* like ones. We're either small like you, fat like me, or skinny like Kevin or Rob. Coach Prescott doesn't know how good we are. He hasn't even given us a chance. Sandy is right, he's just rejected us. Thrown us away."

"Well, I'm going to show him. When I get on the field." David pursed his lips.

"You mean if you get on the field," said Patrick.

"We will. He's an ex-pro. He just has a different system, that's all," David insisted.

"David's right, we'll just have to play hard and show old Prescott what we can do. 'A positive attitude will go a long ways' my dad says," Kevin said.

"Maybe," Rob unfolded his long limbs, stood up and stretched.

"Easy for you guys to say. I ain't getting to play goalie, so how am I going to show my stuff?" Patrick turned away from the other boys.

The whistle blew again.

"Well, that's half-time. Anyone want to bet — do we get to play or not?" Rob turned and loped towards the coach.

They got to play. To be on the field. To show their stuff. But fate was against them.

David stood paralyzed as the world switched to slow-mo. He watched the ball arc slowly through the air. He watched it bounce towards Patrick. He saw Patrick automatically dive and grab the ball. He heard himself cry out. "Oh, Patrick. NO." Then the whistle blew and time was back to normal.

"You BRAINLESS BORG. Are you programmed for only one thing? You're the sweeper now, not the goalie. Keep your hands off the ball." Sandy's freckled face was nose to nose with Patrick's.

For a moment Patrick stood there, red faced, head hanging. Then he gave a little shiver, squared his shoulders and looked straight into Sandy's hazel eyes.

"Sorry. Good habits are hard to break." He turned and sauntered over to David.

"What a jerk. You've saved his butt a gazillion times already this half." David gave the goalie a dirty look.

"No big deal, Davie, my man. We all make mistakes." Patrick glanced over his shoulder. "Some of us more than others."

How true that was. Unbelievably, the three-three tie of the first half had held. No thanks to Sandy though. Every time the Falcons shot, Sandy froze, and they scored. Luckily, they had only had three shots on goal. But then, both teams were playing poorly. Opening night jitters, the coach had said.

Patrick had fouled with one minute left on the clock. What bad luck — a direct kick from just outside the box. A chance for the Falcons to go ahead.

The kicker took his place before the ball. The Hornets formed "the wall" in front of Sandy and glared at Patrick as they passed him. Myles squeezed in between David and his friend, elbowing Patrick in the ribs.

"That's to help you learn the rules, porky," he said.

The referee blew the whistle. The Falcon player kicked the ball. It whipped between two Hornets and headed straight for Sandy. He froze for a second, then dove for the ball. It bounced off his shins right into the goal.

The whistle sounded. First game over. Falcon cheers drowned out the Hornets' groans.

The boys dragged their feet over to the bench.

"Okay lads, lets give our opponents a hearty cheer," Prescott said.

The boys made a circle.

"Move, jerk face. Go stand by some other loser." Myles muscled Patrick out of the circle. Green eyes glaring.

"A-firmative." Sandy closed in the gap and placed his arm on Myles's shoulder.

"Something always goes wrong," said Rob, making room for Patrick in the huddle between David and himself.

The team mumbled, "Falcons, Falcons, hip-hip-hurrah."

"Come on lads, you can do better than that."

"Falcons. Falcons. HIP-HIP-HURRAH!"

"Now, go out there and shake hands." Prescott tousled Sandy's blond hair. "Chin up, Jocko. You'll do better next time."

"It's a good thing for you we don't have to shake hands with dorks on our own team. I'd break all the bones in your mitts." Myles pretended to squeeze an imaginary hand. "Crack. Crack. Crack."

"That's one way to make sure *Fingers* will keep his hands off the ball!" Sandy began to laugh.

"Come on, Patrick. I'll get Mom to spring for cold drinks." David pulled his friend off the field as soon as he shook the last hand.

* * *

"I'm doomed. The season might as well be over. I showed old Prescott all right." Patrick stabbed at his slushie with his straw.

"Get real, Patrick. It was only one play. You made a dozen good ones, too." David slurped on his drink.

"It's the only one they'll remember, though. Myles and his gang are already calling me 'Fingers.' You heard them."

"Forget it. They're just mean. Hey, I thought of something." David started to giggle. "They couldn't ever call Sandy 'Fingers.' His hands never touched the ball."

Patrick cracked a smile.

"Poor guy, he sucked didn't he? Coach Prescott was real great about it, too. Maybe he's not so bad. Maybe he'll forgive my mistake. Got to go Davie." He raised his drink in a salute to David, then took off in a jog down the sidewalk.

David picked up his soccer ball and headed for the driveway.

Swish. Thump. Dribble. Stop. Swish, thump, dribble, stop. David's body fell in to the rhythm of the ball. Kick the ball. Plant the feet. Stop the rebound. Kick again. This is great, he thought. Almost like folk dancing in gym class.

He started to get silly. Kick the ball. Step to the right. Raise the left foot. Stop the ball. Step to the left. Kick the ball. David started to giggle. Lost his footing. Lost the rhythm. The ball rolled onto the grass. He flopped down beside it, laughing. He rolled onto his stomach, pulled the ball towards him and rested his chin on it.

David closed his eyes. He could hear the clatter of dishes through the kitchen window. The aroma of perking coffee drifted on the breeze. It mixed with the scent of juniper bushes — tugging at his memories. Last year, David, Mom, and Gramps all went camping together. All that was missing was the sound of the brook that ran through the campsite.

He sighed. Those were good times. Gramps couldn't have changed so much. Determined, he marched into the kitchen. Poured a cup of coffee. And headed for Gramps' room.

David shifted from one foot to the other, careful not to spill the hot brown liquid. His peace offering. He rubbed his free hand on the front of his shirt, wiping off the sweat. Then he knocked on the door hesitantly.

There was no answer.

He took a deep breath and knocked louder. "Gramps, it's me David."

"Oh, for pete's sake. Come in, if you have to."

Too late now to change his mind. He held the mug out towards his grandfather.

"I brought you some coffee, Gramps."

"I can get my own coffee if I want some. I'm quite capable of looking after myself. I'm not an invalid."

"I know, Gramps, but Mom just made a pot and it smelled of good times — you know like breakfast in the mountains. Anyway ... I thought you would like some."

He placed the rejected offering on the table beside the old man. Then he turned to leave. He almost didn't hear the gruff "thanks," but he did. David's smile widened.

5

On the Defence

I don't know about you guys, but I've had enough. I'm not dribbling this thing any more." Patrick picked up his ball and chucked it.

"What are you going to do?" David walked over to his friend. The rest of the boys followed.

"Know what I want? I want a game. I'm loosing my touch as goalie, Davie, I can feel it."

"Oh, no, not you, Patrick. You can save most of my shots."

"No offense, but saving all the shots in your driveway just doesn't cut it, Davie. I need the game. I need the other team. To be able to figure out the right moves, I need at least a scrimmage. I don't know why. I just do." Patrick turned to the other boys. "Four against four. Who's up for it?"

"Guess I'll play — doesn't really matter what we do," Rob answered.

David glanced nervously across the field. "Maybe, we should do some other drills. You know, ones we learned from last year's coach. Coach Prescott couldn't possibly mind. He wouldn't get mad."

"Good idea, Davie, maybe next time. Today we play, right guys? Four against four." Patrick looked at David. "Are you in or out?"

David hesitated — but only for a moment. Then he nodded. "I'm in."

"All right! Today the Rejects break free. Those two trees are your goal and the bush and that tree is *mine*. I'm in goal." Patrick jogged down to his end whistling.

The ball dropped. The air became alive with the sounds of boys enjoying themselves.

A couple of times David gave an uncertain glance towards Coach Prescott and the other group. But they were busy doing their own thing, oblivious of what was taking place on the other side of the field. Even when the coach blew his whistle to end the practice, his only comment was, "Game Wednesday against the Coyotes, Saint Vital Park, seven-fifteen. Be there a half hour before the game."

"Now, Davie, *that* was fun." Patrick wiped the sweat off his forehead with his sleeve.

"Yeah." David squirted himself with his water bottle.

"Give me a squirt. Sure could use a slushie," Patrick said.

"No kidding. I'll ask Mom, she's always game," David said as he sprayed his friend.

"Well, boys, how'd it go?" David's mother asked.

"Just great, Mom. A real workout." David slid into the back seat.

"You both look pooped. How about a cold one? My treat."

"You read my mind, Mrs. DeMarco. You must be psychic." Patrick piled in beside David.

"Did Coach Prescott teach you any more of his professional secrets?" His mom put the car in gear.

"Nope not today. Other group's turn," David replied quickly.

Patrick jabbed his friend with his elbow and gave him a look that said 'what gives?'

"Tell you later," David mouthed back.

He hadn't told his mother about being one of the Rejects. And he wasn't going to. Things had been hard enough at home. He wasn't about to tell her that soccer wasn't all he had hoped it would be. Especially after she had argued with Gramps about him playing. If he was lucky, she would never find out.

That night he lay in bed tired but satisfied. Glad that Patrick had suggested a scrimmage. Glad that the Rejects had enjoyed a practice for a change. But most of all — he smiled from ear to ear — glad that they had rejected Prescotts' plans.

He rolled over and snuggled under the covers. He couldn't wait for tomorrow. Game day.

* * *

"Okay, the salad and casserole are in the fridge. Microwave the tuna for ten minutes. I think there should be enough milk for supper. I'll bring some home after work tonight — better write that down."

David's mother pulled out her pink daybook from her old black purse. She flipped to the correct date. "Oh, no. I knew I was forgetting something. David you have a game tonight. Dad —"

"Hey, don't look at me." Gramps raised the newspaper protectively in front of him.

"Please, Dad, I need your help." His mom reached over and pulled the paper out of his hands.

"Aw, Shirley, you know I didn't want any part of this soccer thing. I'd take him to music — you know I would."

"I'm not asking you to enjoy it, Dad. I'm asking you to drive him. That's why we moved in together. I help you, you help me." She ran her fingers through her hair.

"Don't you try and twist things, missy. I agreed to move in to help with the expenses. I didn't need help —"

"Dad that's not true and you know it."

Another fight. He didn't want another fight.

"It's okay, Mom. I was going to walk by myself. It's just at the park — we're home team," David blurted out.

"David, you can't go alone. For heaven's sake. You know I don't like you going to the park by yourself, especially in the evening."

"I'll call Patrick. I'll go with him. Please, Mom, please."

"Okay, but if you don't have someone to go with, you can't go. That's final. I don't have time to argue. I'm going to be late for work." She grabbed her white sweater and blew David a kiss.

David picked up the phone and dialed. He counted the rings.

"Four ... five ... six."

The answering machine clicked on. He waited for the beep.

"Patrick, it's me, David. Want to go to the game together? If your parents won't let you take your bike, can I get a ride?"

He sat down beside the phone and waited. Five minutes. Ten minutes. Should he call someone else? Kevin? Rob? But they both lived on the other side of the park. Myles lived close. Maybe he should call him? Naw, he'd rather stay home than ask that snob for a favour.

David moved to the organ and practiced half-heartedly.

"So what time is your friend coming, then?" Gramps shifted his weight in the old plaid chair to face David.

"I don't know. He hasn't called back yet. We don't have to be there till six-thirty, though."

His grandfather pulled out his old pocket watch and squinted at it.

"Five o'clock, best have some supper, son."

David toyed with his tuna, picking off the crunchy topping and popping it into his mouth.

"Something wrong with the casserole?" His grandfather forked up a mouthful.

"I'm not hungry, Gramps."

"You need energy for that game of yours. Tell you what, I saw some pudding in the fridge. Quick energy. How about some of that?" Gramps spooned two heaping bowls of vanilla pudding. "You know what this needs? A nice dollop of jam."

He reached up into the cupboard and pulled out the jam. For a few minutes he struggled with the lid.

"Aw, for crying out loud." He shoved the jar away. It slid across the counter crashing into the sugar canister.

"Can't even open a measly jam jar." He stood looking at his hands.

"Here, Gramps, let me try." With a quick twist David opened the jar. "I guess you loosened it."

"No, son, these stupid hands — arthritis. Fine one day, swollen and painful the next. Never know when they're going to let me down."

"I know what you mean Gramps. It's like my asthma. A pain isn't it?"

David swirled the jam into the white pudding. Then choosing his words carefully, he said, "Is that why you moved in with us, Gramps?"

"Partly."

"You don't like it here much, do you?"

"Don't get me wrong, David. I'm not ungrateful, but a man needs his independence. I've lived on my own for the last eight years. I ate where I wanted, slept when I wanted. Got set in my ways, I guess. Don't like too much change any more. I get cranky."

"Hmm." David stuffed the last spoonful of pudding into his mouth. "I'd better get ready for the game."

He'd started up the stairs two at a time when the phone rang.

"I'll get it." He slid down the banister and grabbed the receiver. "Hello?"

The line went dead. Wrong number.

David climbed back up the stairs. He changed. Then he went outside to wait, listening carefully, in case the phone rang in the house.

"You still here?" Gramps lowered himself onto the top step beside David. "Where's your pal?"

"I don't think he's coming." David stared at his feet.

"Well, what did he say when he called?"

"He didn't call. It was a wrong number."

"Oh. So, now what?" Gramps pushed his cap back on his head.

"I guess I can't go."

"Tell you what. You can walk to the park with me. I planned on going to feed the ducks once you left anyway."

"You mean it Gramps? Oh, thank you." He wanted to hug his grandfather, like he did in the old days, but he held back.

"We'd better hurry so you'll get there before the game starts." Gramps pulled himself up by the wrought iron railings. He took off at a brisk pace with David jogging beside him.

"Don't forget to meet me back here after the game," Gramps called at David's back. Then he pinched a lump of bread off a crust and tossed it to the mallards.

David cut through the bushes and ran over to the soccer field. He searched for Patrick among the gold and black figures crowding around the coach. He wasn't there.

"... Myles, you're center and of course, Sandy, you're in goal. Get your shirt and gloves on. Okay lads, hustle out there."

"Guess we're the spares again." David flopped down beside Kevin and Rob to wait out the first half.

"I wonder where Patrick is? He's never missed a game. Kind of like Bob Cameron of the Winnipeg Blue Bombers — played two hundred and ninety-three games in a row." Kevin brushed back his taffy-coloured hair with his hand.

"Maybe he quit. After the last game he was really down," Rob answered.

"Patrick's not a quitter. Hey, there he is."

David pointed to a figure jogging around the field to avoid interfering with the game. When he reached Coach Prescott, he stopped.

"Sir, Coach, I'm here — Patrick. Patrick Metzler."

"You're late." The coach wrote something on his clipboard.

"Sorry sir, but —"

"No excuses. I asked you to be here a half hour before game time and you can't even show up before the game starts. You'll sit this one out, and that's that." Prescott turned his back to Patrick and focused his attention on the game.

Head hanging, feet dragging, Patrick made his way to the others.

"Great. No playing goalie, no coaching and now I can't even be a few minutes late."

"Where were you? I called," David asked.

"Dentist — lost a filling on a stupid jaw-breaker. See." Patrick opened his mouth wide and pointed to the offending tooth. "This side of my face still doesn't feel right."

"Hey, look. Myles has a breakaway ... figures, he missed the open net." Rob hit his forehead with the palm of his hand.

The momentum of the game suddenly picked up. David was back on his feet, pacing the sidelines. This was more like it. The action was up and down the field — two equally matched teams playing well. A real defensive game. Even Sandy had made a save or two — nothing spectacular, but saves none the less. By half time, only one ball had dribbled past him. The Hornets, however, hadn't been able to score.

They sprawled on the grass resting, waiting for the ref to blow the whistle that ended the break. The coach called out line changes to the team. Rejects were subbed off by those who had sat out the first half. That is, all except poor Patrick. He definitely wasn't being allowed to play. The coach's pets, on the other hand, would be playing the whole game — again.

"Hey, Davie. Figured out the pro's system yet?" Patrick elbowed his friend.

David's face reddened. He didn't reply. So, when the ref's whistle sounded he was relieved to go out on the field.

When play resumed, the energy level was still high. David found himself caught up in the spirit, diving into the melee, heedless of the size of his opponents. More than once he squeezed his tiny body in among a knot of brown and white, forcing the ball loose. It looked like they were going to have to settle for a second loss when Rob kicked a real blooper. It bounced off of Myles' dark head, right into the goal as the final whistle blew. Myles did a victory dance like a football pro; he acted like the header was intentional. The Hornets went crazy, high-fiving and slapping backs.

"Way to go, Myles. Nice header. Way to go, lad," Prescott yelled. He grabbed the game ball and tossed it high in the air.

6

Breakfast, Brunch, and Balderdash

"David, look. It's Coach Rooda. Let's go say 'hi.'" Patrick took off.

David glanced up. Over the shelves that separated the aisles, he caught a glimpse of the bald head of his coach from last year. The man had just started to walk towards the check-outs. David hesitated only long enough to shove the comic book back into the stand. Then he ran also. He had to swerve to miss bumping into his friend. Patrick had skidded to a stop and was backing up slowly.

"Wha —" David started to speak but was silenced by his friend's stern look.

Once Patrick was hidden by the shelves again, he pointed for David to look around the corner.

David peeked. All he saw was Coach Rooda at the end of a long line of people waiting to pay for their items.

"What?" David arched his eyebrows.

"Look again," Patrick whispered back.

David stuck his head out cautiously. This time he saw that his old coach was speaking to someone. Someone hidden by the free standing Mother's Day display. The line moved. Rats. Double rats. Coach Prescott came into view. No wonder Patrick had stopped dead.

"How's the team shaping up?" David heard Mr. Rooda say.

"Not bad, not bad at all," Prescott answered.

"You've got a good core of players from last year. No stars, mind you. Just plain good guys. Hard workers — real diggers. They'll give you one hundred and ten percent. If the new guys mesh, you'll have a good chance at the championship." Rooda patted Prescott on the shoulder.

"Aye, there are some great lads there. Well built."

"You can bet he's not talking about us." Patrick puffed out his cheeks to make himself look as fat as he could. Then he sucked them in, trying his best to look thin.

"Shut up." David wanted to hear what the men were saying. He was praying Coach Rooda would tell Prescott that Patrick, David and the rest of the Rejects were the good guys, but he didn't.

"The lads remind me of me and my mates when we were that age." Prescott was smiling — all misty eyed. "Everywhere we went we played soccer ..."

"My friends and I played baseball. Didn't get into soccer until my kid wanted to —"

Prescott continued as if the other man hadn't spoken. "It made no difference whether we were kicking a tin can on the road or a ball down the field. We gave it everything we had." Coach Prescott sighed, paused for a moment, then started again. "Those were the days. When I was eleven, I had a growth spurt and joined the ranks of the tall and strapping. With my mates' help, I made the Baker Street Bulldogs — an elite soccer club. I was unsure of myself — shy, retreating. That lad, Sandy, reminds me of myself. Good coaching that year was the making of me."

"Sheesh, the idiot thinks he's Sandy." Patrick rolled his eyes.

"You mean, he thinks Sandy's him." David corrected his friend.

"Whatever. No wonder Sandy's his pet."

"But he's not shy."

"Course not. It's all in Prescott's head." Patrick pointed a finger to his temple and traced circles. "Coo-coo."

"There were four of us. We all wanted to play pro when we grew up." Prescott gave a chuckle and a wink. "But first, of course, we would play for Britain in the Olympics. After all, we were like the Union Jack — a little of each part of the kingdom. There was our leader, Rory — black Irish."

"Poor Coach Rooda, he has to listen to this crap." Patrick stopped. David wasn't paying any attention to him. He was focused on the coaches' conversation.

"Dark hair — does he mean Myles?" David asked in a murmur.

Patrick began paying attention, too.

"Then there was Gareth. His father was Welsh. Ah, Stuart that carrot-top Scott ..." Prescott continued.

"James and Tyler?" David asked.

"Tyler for sure — carrot-top. I don't know what a Welsh kid looks like."

Coach Prescott had reached the front of the line. He handed the cashier his purchases, paid, then he turned back to Mr. Rooda.

"What a year that was. What a team. Too bad my dad got transferred to Manchester. I lost touch with the lads. Ah, what a year. We did our coach proud." Prescott sighed.

"I'm sure this team will do you proud, Colin, like they did me." Coach Rooda finally got a word in.

"No doubt, no doubt." Prescott smiled. He waited for Mr. Rooda to pay for his things. Then they walked out together.

"Seems like the jerk is always spoiling our fun. Oh, well. Better pick up a card for my mom or else she'll be unhappy tomorrow," Patrick said. "Got yours yet?"

David nodded yes.

* * *

David stared out the window at Uncle Jake and his friend struggling with the piano. They were unloading it from a moving van. Gramps was yelling orders while Mom was chewing her nails, trying to stay out of the way. This was the strangest Mother's Day that he could remember.

Usually, he got up before his mother and made her breakfast. He had done this since he was six years old. The idea had come from a story that his grade one teacher had read them. He smiled as he remembered that first breakfast — burnt toast, slathered with peanut butter and grape jelly. He must have used half the jar of jelly. A bowl of dry Cheerios. No milk, because David wasn't fond of the stuff. He only drank it because he had to. And the beverage? A cup of warm tap water with a heaping spoon of coffee. He chuckled at his first venture into cooking. Poor Mom.

Later he had discovered that she didn't care for peanut butter. He realized how much his mother loved him because she had finished it all — every sticky, mouth coating bite. His breakfasts were better now. Mom had taught him to cook using the microwave.

This morning he had awoken to the sound of the doorbell ringing. Mom was up. Gramps was up. By the time he'd come downstairs, his Aunty May, was in the living room. Her husband, Uncle Jake, hadn't been with her.

"What's up?" he'd asked.

"We're delivering your grandma's piano to the house today," Aunty May had said as she'd lowered her plump body into a chair. "The truck should be along any minute now."

"Why today? Why now?" David had wanted to know. That wasn't the way it was supposed to be.

"Because it's the only time that your uncle's friend could borrow the moving van from his boss," Mom had said.

"Mustn't look a gift horse in the mouth, David." His aunt had shook her head at him. The blue-black feather in her hat had bobbed in unison.

"But what about breakfast?"

His disappointment must have been obvious, but his aunt had misunderstood the reason.

"Hungry, are we? Not to worry. We are all going out to brunch once the piano is installed. A big boy like you can wait that long."

Brunch. That explained why she was all dressed up. That explained the dorky hat perched on her brassy hair.

David felt cheated. There would be no special gift from him to his mother. Oh, he had bought her a scarf — silk, with pink and blue swirls. But it was the breakfast that was the special gift.

Brunch. Ha. All la-di-da like Aunty May. Robbing him of his gift. Breakfast, that's what it was. Breakfast. What else could it be at nine in the morning

"Hey, be careful." Gramps' yell brought David back to earth. Uncle Jake had stumbled on a crack in the sidewalk.

With a bit of a struggle the piano was delivered into the living room. The front door had to be removed to get it in the house.

"Shirley, where do you want us to put it," Uncle Jake asked.

"Gee, I'm not sure. I figured if we put the chair over here it should fit against that wall," his mom replied.

David wasn't sure he liked the change. He wouldn't be able to sprawl in the chair to watch TV any more. In its new spot, the angle was wrong. Oh, well. Just one more change in a year full of them. He couldn't figure out why they needed the piano anyway. There was an organ in the house already.

"Well? What do you think, Dad? Would she approve? Her piano safe, in a place of honour in my home. A Mother's Day gift to her memory." David's mother stood with her arm around Gramps.

He just grunted his approval as he wiped away a tear.

These last two weeks, Gramps and Mom had spent most of her time off packing up things at the old house. David had thought that Uncle Jake had somehow convinced the old man to sell the place. But that wasn't it. Mom had told him that one of her cousins was moving back to Winnipeg. Her husband had lost his job, so they couldn't afford to stay in Toronto any more. Gramps had offered to let them stay in the house until they were back on their feet. Good for Gramps.

David felt happy for his grandfather. He could still keep his home. There would be family living in it. Just like he said he wanted.

7

Where There's Smoke

David looked up in surprise. Gramps stood in the doorway. He seldom came upstairs and he had never come into David's room since moving in.

"Where does your mother keep the ashtrays? I've looked high and low and I can't find the darn things."

"There aren't any. Mom gave them to Goodwill last fall. She said we didn't need ashtrays in a smoke-free house," David replied.

"Well, my friend needs a cigarette. I guess he can use a saucer."

"Gramps, Mom doesn't let anyone smoke in the house."

"Tough. She'll just have to adjust. After all, she insisted I move here. This is my home now, so if my friend wants to smoke he can."

"But, Gramps, I'm —"

"Look David, this is none of your business. I'll deal with your mother." Gramps turned and walked away.

I wish he'd just let me finish speaking, thought David. He turned back to his homework and tried to concentrate. He had almost completed the math questions when he detected a hint of cigarette smoke in the air. David opened his window wide. He then went to his closet and pulled out the fan that was stored there. He pointed it towards the door and turned it on. Maybe it would blow the smoke out of his room.

David started to sniff. The gunk in the back of his throat forced him to cough, violently and incessantly. He decided to leave the house. But first he needed some antihistamine. He took the cough syrup out of the medicine cabinet. David read the label carefully, then tried to pour the correct dosage into the tiny cup. On the third try he got it. He'd never done this before. Except for his inhaler, an adult had always given him any medication he needed. He should have called Gramps, but he was afraid to bother him.

Once outside, David sat down on the front stairs and took his inhaler. His chest was tight. He needed a drink but he didn't want to re-enter the smoky house. Turning on the garden tap, he stuck his mouth in the stream of water and took quick, cold gulps. Satisfied, he wiped his mouth on his sleeve.

Where to now? Go visit Patrick? No. He wasn't allowed to leave the house without telling someone. He settled for the next best thing — his retreat. The tree house.

Slowly the coughing eased. Then stopped. But his chest hurt from the hacking and he felt weak. He rested his head against the rough log walls, closing his eyes for a minute. When he opened them again, he found himself looking into the kitchen. Funny he had never noticed this knothole in the logs before. It gave him a perfect view into the room.

"Hey, Joe, want a cup of coffee?" Gramps called over his shoulder as he came into sight.

Boy, with the window open you could hear everything so clearly.

"Don't mind if I do," his grandfather's friend replied, his voice harsh and gravelly.

For a second David watched Gramps spoon the grounds into the coffee maker. Then he turned his attention to Joe. Stickman, he thought. A bag of bones that threatened to fall apart every time he coughed. And cough he did. Often. Explosive, gut wrenching coughs. Man, he's as bad as me when my asthma is acting up. And yet he smokes. There was a cigarette between his lips continuously. As he butted out one, he lit another. The saucer in front of him was overflowing.

The house would reek. Maybe the old man would leave soon.

But he didn't. David could wait no longer. He decided to open all the windows in the house to clear the air. Then he figured he'd sit in the tree house till bedtime. No big deal — right?

He inhaled deeply a few times and then ran into the house. His lungs were almost bursting from holding his breath. He'd barely cracked open the first window when he was forced to exhale. He pressed his face against the screen and gulped fresh air.

David forced himself to relax, to focus on the job at hand. Inhale. Fill the lungs. Hold it. Run to the next window. By the time he reached his own room he was wheezing and coughing again. He felt weak. He needed his inhaler once more. He glanced at the clock radio. Only two and a half hours since the last dose. He normally took his medication every four hours. He had never needed it any earlier. Now what? Then he remembered — the doctor had told his mom that he could take three doses twenty minutes apart if it ever became necessary. Should he? Yeah, he needed the stuff. He used his inhaler.

David turned the fan back on. He pulled a chair to the window and sat there, face glued to the screen. Waiting. Waiting for the medicine to work. Waiting for Joe to leave. No luck.

Twenty minutes later he needed another dose. He took it.

Tears rolled down his cheeks. He wished his mother was home — but she was on the three to eleven shift. As he lifted his hand to swipe at the tears, he noticed his fingers were shaking. He tried to control them, but he couldn't. Panicked, he ran downstairs to call Gramps. Near the bottom his legs buckled. He grabbed the banister and sunk onto the step.

Joe walked out of the bathroom. Seeing David, the old man shuffled over and bent down to get a closer look — coughing tobacco breath at him. David coughed, too. His lungs hurt.

"Hey — the kid don't look so good. Get in here," Joe yelled over his shoulder.

Gramps pushed past Joe. "Oh lord, you look awful. Take your puffer."

"I did. It hasn't helped much. And I'm shaking. I can't stop shaking." David held out his hand so they could see.

"Oh lord, better do something, man. Call a doctor. Call an ambulance. Do something real fast." Joe stood there wringing his hands.

"Shut up, Joe. Come on. Can you walk? Let's go. I'm taking you to the hospital." Gramps put his arms around David and pulled him to his feet. "Here. Lean on me."

They hobbled towards the door. Gramps grabbed his cap from the hall closet. He patted his pocket.

"Oh, hell. Joe, fetch my keys from my dresser. And Joe, please leave a note for Shirley telling her where we've gone." Gramps snatched the keys from his friend. "Thanks. Lock up when you leave."

"Blast it!" Gramps had trouble inserting the key into the ignition. Finally, they squealed out of the driveway. They honked and swerved their way down Bishop Grandin Highway. David was afraid that his grandfather would run a red light. He had never seen the old man so panicked. Gramps half dragged, half carried him into the emergency department.

"Nurse, nurse, help him. He can't breathe. We need a doctor now." He grasped hold of the reception nurse's arm.

"Calm down, sir. Here take a seat." She waved David into a seat at the admitting desk. "Your name, please?"

"David. David DeMarco."

"Mr. DeMarco, may I have your medical card please?" She held out her hand to Gramps.

Oh, oh. The last time someone had called him that he had gotten very angry. The poor meter reader had almost run from the house. But Gramps didn't even blink. He pulled out his card and handed it to the lady.

"Sir, the boy's not on this card."

"Of course not. He's my grandson."

"Sir, we need his number. Could I have *his* card, please?"

"Oh my lord. I don't have his card. I didn't think of his card. What am I going to do? He needs a doctor."

"Take it easy, sir. Don't worry. We'll take care of the boy. Just calm down." She turned to David. "Son, have you ever been here before?"

"Yes, last fall — September, I think. When they were burning stubble," David answered.

"Okay. Now we're cooking." She typed his name into the computer.

"Your address is three-twenty Saint Michael Street?"

"Yes," he replied.

"Good." She quickly took down his information off the screen.

"Now tell me the problem."

"It's my asthma. I've taken my inhaler three times already. It's not helping. And I'm shaking. See." Once again David held out his hand to show his trembling fingers.

The nurse gently took his hand and attached a clip to his finger as he spoke. It looked like a clothespin attached by a cord to a box. The black box gave a digital read out.

"What are you doing to him?" Gramps asked.

"It's okay. She's just getting my blood oxygen level," David assured him.

"Do you remember when you first started experiencing difficulties?" She peered over her glasses.

David stared at the changing digits on the instrument for a moment. He gave a sigh.

"It was around five-thirty. That's when I took the inhaler for the first time. Then I took it at eight, and again at eight-twenty. That's when I started shaking." His brown eyes were worried.

"Are you allergic to anything?"

"Yes, a whole bunch of plants and ..." he hesitated. He didn't want to upset Gramps.

"And?" the nurse coaxed.

"Tell her, son. She needs to know." Gramps squeezed David's shoulders.

"Tobacco. Tobacco smoke."

"David, for crying out loud. Why didn't you tell me?"

"I tried, Gramps, but you wouldn't listen."

"Oh lord, it's my fault. I didn't know. I'm sorry, David. I'm sorry."

"He's going to be just fine, sir. His blood oxygen isn't too bad." She pointed at the readout. "See. Come on, David."

They followed her down the hall to a small room.

"Here. Take off your shirt and put on this gown — the opening's in the back. Up you get." The nurse patted the examination table and left.

Through the door they heard her say, "There's a little wheezer in room six, Doc."

It was so quiet. David started to feel uneasy. He glanced around the room to distract himself. There were counters along three walls. Under them were cupboards and open shelves filled with linens, jars and small boxes. At one end was a sink. Almost everything was white — even the walls. On them hung strange looking gadgets. He recognized a number of them — the blood pressure cuff, the thingy the doctor used to look into eyes and ears and the container to dispose of hazardous materials. Just behind him, in a tangle of hoses, hung the equipment that was used to deliver medication to people with breathing problems. He had used it the last time he was here.

Gramps was still standing, staring at the closed door. His arms were hanging down in front of him. The knuckles on his fingers were turning white from squeezing the peak of his cap too tight.

"Gramps, do you want to sit down?" he asked the old man. "There's a chair in the corner by the sink."

"Huh? Oh." His grandfather dragged the chair over to the padded table on which David sat. He lowered himself into the chair, eyes still glued to the door, silently waiting.

The silence was overpowering. David broke it.

"Did you play soccer as a kid, Gramps?"

"Sure. I kicked the ball around the school yard with my pals."

"Did you like it?"

"It was okay, I suppose."

David's face fell.

"Don't look so glum. In my day, soccer wasn't big. Baseball was. Had great eye-hand coordination — still do for that matter. When you were a rug rat, I would play in old timer's tournaments. Sure miss it. Lousy arthritis."

Gramps lapsed into silence again, his head hanging down. He looked sad.

"I don't know much about baseball, Gramps. We could go to a Goldeyes' game together? You could teach me about the sport."

"I'd like that. Can't remember the last time I went to a game with a kid. Must have been when your Uncle Jake was a teenager. We used to go to Minneapolis once a summer to take in the Twins. There were no pro teams in Winnipeg then. I coached Jake's ball team, too. Started coaching him when he was younger than you. Sure miss those days."

"You know, Gramps, if you really miss baseball so much, why don't you help coach a little league team at the community club? They're always looking for help."

"Now that's an idea. Maybe I'll do just that." His grandfather turned to see who was entering the room.

"Hello. Doctor Monteiro." He held out his hand to shake Gramps'. He turned to David. "Well, young man — having a little trouble breathing, are we? Let's take a look."

The doctor placed a stethoscope on David's back. "Take a deep breath."

The process was repeated up his back and down his front.

"Not bad. Looks like your inhaler is doing its job." He jotted something on the chart.

The doctor was right. Sometime during the wait, the coughing had stopped, also, he was hardy wheezing anymore.

"Just to be on the safe side, we'll give you a dose of ventalin in a mask. The nurse will be along in a minute to set you up." He turned to leave.

"Hold on there, young fella. What about the shakes?" Gramps asked.

David blushed. You didn't call doctors young fellow, no matter how old you were. But he was glad Gramps asked, because the shaking hadn't stopped.

"The shakes?" Doctor Monteiro raised his bushy black eyebrows.

"The kid's hands are trembling like leaves. Show him David," his grandfather said.

David stretched his hands out in front of him.

"Oh, that. Ventalin is a stimulant. Tremors can be a side effect."

"It's never happened before. Man, was I scared."

"Well, now you know. Cheer up, we're going to be tip-top." He chucked David under the chin and was off.

* * *

David was shivering. He hadn't noticed how cool the evening had become when he'd left for the hospital. He had just been too worried. He huddled close to Gramps as the old man unlocked the front door.

"Lord, I'm bushed." His grandfather put an arm around him. "Come on. Let's get you to bed."

David stumbled into the house. It felt as cold as outside. He shivered again as a draft blew across his face. Geez, Joe had left the windows opened when he had locked up. He started to close them. Oh well, at least the cigarette smoke was gone.

"What are you doing awake? My gosh. It's almost midnight."

David jumped. Mom. She had walked into the house without him hearing.

"We only got back from the hospital a few minutes a —"

"Hospital!" His mom cut him off. "What happened?"

"Just my asthma, Mom."

"Dad, why in heaven's name didn't you call me?" She threw her purse on the couch and turned on Gramps.

"Shirley, I didn't think. You're right. I should have called you. What can I say? All I wanted to do was to get the boy to emergency. He put his hands on her shoulders. "Forgive me?"

She shrugged off his hands.

"Please, Mom, don't get mad. Everything's okay now. Gramps took good care of me." David gave a big yawn. All he wanted to do was drag himself to bed. "Can't I go to sleep now?"

"Of course, honey." She walked over to him and gave him a hug. She planted a kiss on his forehead. "Goodnight, love."

8

Invisible Ally

The ball bounced right in front of David. He never even noticed. He was too busy watching Gramps. All evening his eyes were drawn to that spot on the dike. The grassy slope made natural bleachers for the field. There his grandfather sat with his mom. Why was he still there? Why hadn't Gramps left to meet his friends? The game was almost over.

The picture of Gramps — walking into the kitchen adjusting his cap — was still clear in David's mind.

"Okay. Let's go," he had said.

David had looked at his mother, but she only raised her eyebrows and shrugged.

"David's got a game tonight. I'm going with him," she told Gramps.

"I know that. It's at the Flood Bowl, right?"

David couldn't believe his ears. His heart started to pound. He crossed his fingers and dared to hope. Gramps next words put a stop to that. Quickly.

"That's just around the corner from my old stomping grounds. Thought I'd go visit some of the old gang. Haven't seen them much since moving here. Might even stop in at the old house and see how your cousin Sadie's doing."

"Oh … okay. I'll drop David off first. Then I'll take you where you want to go. But I'm going back to watch the game," his mother said.

"No need, Shirley. I'll just walk from the field. Nice evening for a stroll."

But there he was, watching the game. From where David stood, it looked like he was enjoying it too.

"Get on it, Reject, or get out of the way and let someone who knows how to play do the job." Myles elbowed him away from the ball, bringing David back to earth. His face flushed red with guilt. He vowed to concentrate.

David followed Myles up the field. He watched him dribble the ball — deking first one opponent, then the next.

"See how it's done. You Rejects should go ruin some other sport," Myles called over his shoulder.

Rob was yelling, "Myles, I'm open."

Pass it. Pass it. You can't go through the whole team every time. You'll lose it, David thought.

Sure enough, Myles lost the ball. The play was coming back David's way. He forced himself among the navy blue bodies and popped out the ball.

Patrick was right there. He booted it down the field. Myles, waiting in front of the goal, used his body to capture the ball. He kicked. Hard. The ball bounced off the inside of the goal post, over the goalie, and in.

Patrick ran over and high-fived David. They watched Myles do his victory dance.

"What team work, eh, Davie?"

"Yeah! One, two, three." His dark eyes gleamed with pleasure.

As Myles ran by, the boys reached out to congratulate him. He ignored their outstretched hands.

"I did it. I did it. I broke the tie," he yelled to the coach as he passed them.

They watched Coach Prescott give him the thumbs-up. "Well done, lad, well done," he said.

"All by himself too, I'm sure." Patrick turned and walked straight into David. "Oops ... We must be ghosts."

"No kidding. Sandy was right. You can become invisible on the field." But so what? He wasn't playing to be noticed. He was playing for the fun of it. And Gramps was there, wasn't he? Right. He walked back to his position, kicking the grass as he went.

* * *

David decided he wasn't going to say anything about Gramps watching the game. He didn't want to jinx things. His mom and grandfather also acted as if nothing special had happened. It was as if everyone agreed not to bring it up. But something special had happened. Gramps started to come to his games. Faithfully. They would discuss how the games went. They had started talking again. So a few weeks later David was caught by surprise when Gramps' angry voice filtered through the kitchen window.

"What he's doing isn't right."

David tossed the soccer ball onto the grass and sank down on the front stairs. All the familiar feelings came rushing back — churning stomach, tight chest, the desire to hold his breath until the shouting stopped.

Strange, he hadn't felt like this for a while. When had the fighting stopped? When Gramps had started coming to the games? Before that? How had he not noticed? No matter — it was back. What had he done to upset Gramps this time?

"So what if he was a pro, Shirley. He could have invented the game for all I care! He doesn't treat the boys well."

It's not me. It's not me. Gramps is mad at Coach Prescott. A wild desire to run and cheer came over him. He fought for control. He wanted to hear every word. David wished he could see them too, but he knew they'd stop talking if he went into the room. What now? The tree house. Yes. He could look through the knothole right into the kitchen, and they couldn't see him.

He made himself as comfortable as he could. Cheek against rough wood, eyes glued to the hole. He saw them by the sink. Gramps washing dishes, Mom wiping.

"He's a nice man, Dad. So cheerful. Always patting the boys on the back and smiling."

"Yup — that smile. Reminds me of a nurse before she sticks you with the needle."

"Oh, Dad." David's mother hit Gramps, playfully, with the tea towel.

"Seriously, Shirley. I've been keeping track. It's the same eight boys that sit on the sidelines, game after game. Doesn't give them much attention at practice either."

"And how would you know?" His mother poked her index finger, gently, into Gramps' side. "I've dropped him off at his practices and I know I didn't take you."

"I have my ways. I've been watching from the duck pond."

"Why, you old sneak." His mom whacked Gramps with the tea towel again.

David shifted his weight to ease the cramping in his legs. He couldn't believe what he was hearing.

"So what was that 'waste of money' stuff about?" She mimicked Gramps.

"A man can change his mind, can't he?" Gramps placed another plate in the rack to drain.

"Yeah, okay. Tell me what you think you saw." His mother picked up the dish and dried it.

"Well ... he's divided them into two groups and —"

"David told me that. Coach Prescott likes to work with small groups."

"Bull. He only works with the one. The other is left on their own. Oh, he comes once in awhile — to give his goalie practice, or if he needs them for a scrimmage. But, mostly, they're on their own."

"Why hasn't David said anything?" His mother's forehead was creased with a frown.

David took a deep breath. His knuckles whitened as he gripped the wall tighter.

"Can't you guess, Shirley? He's just like you. Believes the best of this world. And, if he finds out different, he keeps quiet so as not to make waves."

"Poor kid. These months haven't been easy for him," his mom said.

"No. No, I suppose not." Gramps wiped his hands on the towel David's mother was holding. "Change is always hard. Look at me. I've been storming around the place like a spoiled child. At my age I should know better. Still, I can't seem to help myself."

"You're lucky he hasn't started calling you Grumps." For just a moment, a weak smile formed on his mom's lips. "As if I should talk — been pretty self-absorbed myself lately. I haven't paid him enough attention. Other things seemed so important. I let staying for his practices become low priority. My mistake."

Her head was bowed, her hands twisting the tea towel. Tears welled in her eyes. She rubbed a finger across them, trying to erase their presence.

"Lord, I'm so tired," she whispered.

Gramps put his arms around her shoulders and pulled her into a bear hug.

"You're a good mother, Shirley. The boy's fine. Like you said, he loves the game. When he's playing he's like a pit bull — focused. As for the practices, the guys are making their own fun."

David dropped back on his heels. It was as if a weight had been lifted from his shoulders, a weight he didn't even know he was carrying. It was good to have everything out in the open.

From then on, Gramps and David started walking to the park together on practice days. Sometimes, Mom would come too. On the home front things were, well, comfortable.

* * *

David crouched behind the bush as Prescott took a step in his direction to pick up another ball.

"Why that blithering idiot." The coach chucked the ball into the mesh bag he was holding. "How dare he tell me how to coach. Who does the old SOB think he is?"

Turn around. Turn around so I can leave, David prayed.

He heard the coach mutter. "I'll teach him to mind his own business. He'll be sorry."

Why had he hidden? Why hadn't he gone back to the car when he'd caught Gramps talking to the coach? If only Gramps had used a better excuse.

"Won't be a minute. Just forgot my cap," he had said.

His mom had sent him after his grandfather when they found it — right there on the front seat. Gramps was already talking to the coach by the time he'd caught up, their backs turned to him.

"Oh, no sir, that can't be. I always sub off two forwards and two defense," Coach Prescott had been saying.

"That may be. But, the same seven kids play the whole game, every game. The other eight kids are doing all the sitting out."

"You must be mistaken."

"No. I've been keeping track. Perhaps it's an oversight. But, if you want them to play as a team, you have to treat them as one team. Kids keep tabs, too, you know. Give them equal playing time. It does wonders for egos. Otherwise, they'll lose interest."

"Thanks for your concern, sir. I'll keep what you said in mind. The lads are my first priority. Wouldn't want to upset anyone, now, would we?" The coach had extended his hand to Gramps, cutting off any further discussion.

His grandfather had grasped Prescott's hand and shook it. He'd started to turn.

That's when David had ducked behind the bush. It had been a reflex. He knew that he wasn't supposed to have heard anything.

Now all he wanted was for the coach to turn around or leave. David could feel a sneeze coming. He held his finger tight against his nose, trying to hold it back.

"I wonder which boy that old codger is attached to." Prescott pulled the neck of the bag tight with an angry jerk.

At that moment David's allergies let him down. He sneezed. The coach stepped towards the bush. David popped up from his hiding place.

"Forgot my … my jacket. Not here. Bye." He turned and ran.

"Hey — boy, hey!"

David pretended he didn't hear. Man, am I glad he hasn't bothered to learn my name, David thought.

He didn't stop running until he reached his mom's red car, heart pounding, palms sweating. He leaned against it for a moment, then jerked open the door.

"Geez, Gramps, where were you. Your cap was in the car all along." He climbed into the back. "Okay, Mom, let's go. NOW."

They turned and looked at him, then, glanced at each other strangely, shaking their heads.

9

On the Offensive

It's not fair. This was our game. We won it — you, me, and the rest of the Rejects. Not Myles. Not Sandy." Patrick chucked his water bottle. The lid popped off spraying David's already wet feet. Patrick was right, of course. It had been their game.

Only three of the coach's pets had been there when David arrived. They'd stood shivering in the cold. Prescott had put his hand on the shoulder of one of them, James — tawny haired and golden skinned.

"We're playing shorthanded. No subs. Unfortunately, most of our best players can't be here."

"Where is everybody?" David wondered out loud.

"Afraid of a little rain," Patrick whispered. The cloudy sky had been threatening all day.

"They're not sick, are they? My dad says there's a bug going around," Kevin asked.

"No, no. Not to worry. They're fine. The Canadian National Soccer Team is in town. They're playing an exhibition game against Brazil. It's an opportunity of a lifetime. I'm glad the lads had this chance to go and watch it."

"Maybe they'll cancel the game," Rob said hopefully. He wiped droplets of rain from his face.

"When have they ever? We're like postmen. Not rain or sleet or snow and however else that saying goes. They'll make us play," Patrick replied.

"You boys will have to give me one hundred and ten percent, nothing less. Right, son?" He reached over and tousled Tyler's red hair. "This is a key game. It determines the quarter-finalists. Don't let the lads down. They fought hard to get us here."

"Yeah, right, like we've been sitting on our butts," David murmured.

"Just like Myles and his gang not to show. If they cared about our team they'd be here." The words were whispered through clenched teeth.

"Oh, Patrick, admit it. You'd have gone, if you'd had the chance," David sighed back.

"Well ... maybe. But, Prescott shouldn't act like they're the whole team."

"Want to play goalie, Tyler? Huh, what do you say, Jocko?" The coach lifted the boy's chin so he could make eye contact.

"Shush, listen." David elbowed his friend in the ribs.

"Oh ... no sir, not me, please. I suck in goal." He shook his head. His white skin paled a shade.

"Let Patrick," a number of the boys said together.

Sensing salvation, Tyler nodded vigorously. "Yes, sir, let him. He's played in goal before."

Coach Prescott's eyes searched the team. "Patrick?"

Patrick stepped forward. The coach looked him over as if checking for flaws. He rubbed his chin.

"I ... don't ... know, James?" He turned to the boy whose shoulder his hand rested on.

"He got us to the championship last year," David couldn't resist blurting.

Prescott's eyes bore into David.

"Hrump. Is that so?"

"Yes, coach, that's true. He really did. Please let him." James' green eyes pleaded too.

Prescott took a deep breath. "Okay, but if he's no good, I'm pulling him. And one of you will have to go in goal."

David, Patrick, Tyler and James gave a communal sigh of relief.

"Well, hop to it. Off with those jackets, lads. Now play a defensive game. Remember, we have no spares."

And what a game they had played. All that dribbling and passing had paid off. Their passes were bang on and the checking was relentless. Patrick, determined to show Prescott, was awesome in goal. He had never played so well in his life.

The air was electric. The rain, light and steady, hadn't hampered either team. By the middle of the second half, the score was three-nothing for the Hornets.

Then the whistle blew and the tide changed.

"What's he calling subs for? There aren't any." Kevin yelled as he tried to dry his glasses with his wet shirt.

"Look who showed up." David pointed to the sidelines.

"Number eleven." Coach Prescott waved him off.

"Guess that's me. See you." David took off at a trot.

"Watch and learn, Reject. See how the big boys do it," Myles sneered as he ran onto the field.

He turned his face into the rain. The droplets dripped down his face and neck. His body, warm from all the running, quickly cooled in the drizzle as he stood on the sideline.

In the goal, Patrick dove to stop a shot. He didn't get up. Prescott ran on the field and helped him off.

"I guess some people can be as late as they like and still not have to sit out a game. While others have to fake injuries because the coach wants Sandy in goal. See? Prescott sent the message 'drop and stay down.' The jerk," Patrick said as he shivered beside David.

"Figures." David struggled into his soggy jacket.

The change in players broke the momentum of the game. The Hornets' passing disintegrated. Desperate to save the lead, Myles went into his one-man team routine. He muscled the ball away from players — it made no difference if they were opponents or teammates. He was unwilling to take a chance on passing, so he held on to the ball too long and he'd loose it.

There were two quick unanswered goals by the Lazers.

"Well, there goes your shutout." David playfully punched Patrick's arm.

As Patrick raised his to swat back, his motion was stopped in midair by David's words.

"Oh my gosh, what's he doing?"

Sandy had come way out of his goal to grab the ball. He almost had it, too. But he slipped on the wet grass and the forward deked around him. All he could do was lie there, helplessly, as the player kicked the ball into the empty net. Tie game, again.

No, not again. Myles got the ball once more and doggedly dribbled through the red and white figures. He lost it. Rob picked it up and inched the ball another few feet, before passing it back to him. A long high boot and the ball went into the goal. Myles did his victory dance. They had just resumed play when the whistle blew to end the game.

Pandemonium broke loose. The Hornets screamed. Wet soggy hugs were exchanged. Coach Prescott ran on to the field. He threw his arm around Myles.

"Way to go, Jocko." He then reached over and pulled Sandy into his hug. "We're in. You lads earned this victory. What would we have done without you?"

Yes, Patrick had been right. It had been their game. But, in fifteen minutes it had been stolen from them — by their own teammates.

"I've had it. Some of the guys are talking about quitting and I think I just might walk with them." Patrick stalked off to his father's car.

Quit? David didn't want to quit. He liked playing. It didn't matter that he didn't like the coach. Anyway, the man pretty much left the Rejects alone — funny how they had adopted that name as their own. Okay, so some kids *always* got to play the whole game, and he didn't ever. It wasn't fair, but hey, the year was almost over.

* * *

The next day at school Patrick asked, "Davie, my man, meeting — Rejects. Saturday. Ten A.M. Can we hold it at your place? No bratty sibs to snoop around. What do you say?"

"Ah … I guess so." What else could he say?

So now, here they were, in his tree house. Packed like sardines.

David closed his eyes and rested his head on the rough logs. Why had he let Patrick hold the meeting at his place? If he had known what the meeting was about, would he have said 'no?' Probably not. Patrick could talk him into anything. But maybe if he tried, he could stop this crazy idea of quitting.

"We quit together, all of us," Patrick announced. "Then Prescott's finished. No chance at the finals. No trophy. Nothing. And the jerk can't do a thing about it."

"We don't have to quit," David said.

But no one heard him. The other boys were too busy laughing and patting Patrick on the back.

"Great idea. What a way to pay the old fart back." Rob shoved Patrick, then added, "If it works."

"But, guys, we're this close to winning the champion-ship," David raised his voice a little. His hands waved in the air for emphasis — his finger and thumb a hair's breath apart.

"I'm with David." Kevin pushed his glasses up with his finger.

"Yeah. Sure would be nice to have a trophy." Adam's elfin face lit up. His fingers, always in motion, tapped the floor beside him.

"Hey, stupid, we're only at the quarter-finals, duh. We could lose, dummy." Rob lightly kicked Adam's small foot.

"Yeah, but we could win," David said.

"Oh, yeah? Well look at last year's playoffs. We lost in the last five minutes. Anything can happen. I say we quit." Jon wiped the chocolate he was eating from his lips.

"But, Prescott played professional soc —" Adam piped up.

"For crying out loud," Patrick cut the boy off. He stuck his finger into his mouth and pretended to gag. "I'm sick of hearing about that. We've lost as many games this season as last year."

"And we've won as many. There's only three games left, guys. I'd like another shot at the championship."

"Well, I'd like a shot at Prescott." Patrick punched into his left palm.

Some of the boys giggled.

"Yeah, let's pay him back." Jon wiped his hands on his jeans.

"But we're shooting for a trophy. My dad says we can win it all," Kevin insisted.

And so it went, round and round.

David had had enough. He tried to block out the voices. They were getting nowhere. He concentrated on the sound of his neighbour's lawn mower. Soon the words blended in with the drone of the motor. He took slow deep breaths, inhaling the scent of newly cut grass. David smiled. It was his favourite smell, that and the smell of freshly cut lumber.

"Hey boys, how about some lemonade?" Gramps' voice cut into his daydreaming.

"All — *right*."

The boys scrambled down the tree-house ladder and swarmed into the kitchen.

"So ... What's the confab about, or is it hush-hush?" Gramps poured the lemonade into tall glasses and passed them around.

"Heck no. Some of us were going to quit the soccer team and we came up with this awesome plan. You tell it Patrick. It was your idea." Jon gulped back his drink and held out his glass for more.

Patrick hesitated, "Hum ... ah ..."

"Go on, son," Gramps squeezed Patrick's shoulder.

"It's like this. The coach treats the Rejects — that's us —" he pointed around the table.

"Like dirt," Rob interrupted.

"Yeah, he doesn't coach us," mumbled Jon around a mouthful.

"He plays his favorite kids all the time." Adam raked his spiked hair with his fingers.

"He's a creep," added Kevin.

"Boys, boys. One at a time. I don't hear as well as I used to. Okay, you were saying?" David's grandfather turned back to Patrick.

"Anyway, we decided if we all quit at the same time that would finish the team. Wouldn't Prescott be sorry then?"

Gramps rubbed his hand across his chin. He stared into space for a moment, then spoke.

"You could be right. But then again, if what you say is true — that he doesn't care a fig about what you do — you might be playing right into his hands."

"Say, what?" Rob's eyes opened wide.

"Well, it's like this: To him you're a nuisance. He has to fit you into his roster when he'd rather be concentrating on the other kids. So, if you quit, good riddance."

"Heck, no way. You can't field a team without nine players," Patrick said.

"Perhaps you're right. Things were different in my days. Mind, I didn't coach soccer, just baseball. Back then, when I was short a player or two, well, I just pulled up the best younger kids I could lay my hands on. Those little guys loved it. Got to play extra games, and with the big boys at that. But that was a long time ago. More lemonade anyone?"

No one answered Gramps. They sat in stunned silence.

David felt like jumping for joy. "He's right, Patrick. Remember last year when half the team had chicken pox? Coach Rooda brought up some nine year olds."

"Aw, rats. Quitting seemed like such a great idea."

"So, now what?" The boys all turned to Patrick.

"Why are you all looking at me?"

"You usually have such cool ideas," Rob answered.

"Well I haven't got one now."

"Think, Patrick, think."

"Knock it off, you twerp." Patrick reached over and swiped at Rob.

"Boys, boys. Stop snarling at each other. Forget about Prescott. Nothing you can do will touch him." Gramps pulled Patrick and Rob apart.

"That's not fair," Jon said as he reached for a banana from the fruit bowl.

"Never said it was, son. But I'll let you in on a secret. People like Prescott don't need you to help them screw up. They manage quite well on their own. It just takes time."

Gramps started to clear the glasses off from the table. He turned back to the boys and spoke again.

"There is something I want you kids to do. Ask yourselves why you joined soccer. When you're on the field, are you getting what you came for? And if you are, do you want to let some moron spoil it for you? How many games are left anyway? Three? Four? Each boy has to answer for himself, then make up his own mind whether to quit or not. Good luck. Now, you best be heading home for lunch."

David watched the door swing shut behind the last boy. He then twirled around, threw his arms about Gramps, and squeezed tightly.

"I love you."

His grandfather chuckled and hugged him back.

"My, my, what did I do to deserve this?" He gently tilted David's head up so he could look into his eyes.

"I want to play soccer."

"Then play."

"But, Gramps, the other boys —"

"Son, are you always going to let others determine what you do?"

10

Cottonwoods and Coaching Calls

David rubbed the tears from his eyes, but his eyes kept watering. His skin stung. The ball had hit him square in the face. The end of his nose felt like it had been whacked by a sledgehammer. Was it broken? He touched it gingerly. No. Only the tip hurt. No bones there.

He wiped the tear that dripped by the side of his nose, then dried his finger on his shirt. It streaked red. He wiped his nose again. Oh no, blood. Rats. Should he try to get the coach's attention and ask for a Kleenex? Heck, no. Prescott would probably pull him. Choosing to play had cost David plenty. No way was he giving up his time on the field.

For three days he'd lived with a knot in his stomach. He had avoided Patrick, afraid his friend would talk him into calling it quits. He'd been sure Patrick would be mad at him for not quitting, but he had worried needlessly. They were all back, the ones that counted, at least — Patrick, Kevin and Rob. Adam who wanted a trophy so badly, stayed as well.

David pinched his nose just below the bone, like his mother had shown him. He took off after the action. It surprised him how much harder it was to play with only one arm free. Maybe the bleeding had stopped. He tested his nose again. His finger remained clean. Excellent. Now he could focus on the game once more. A good thing too, because here came the Falcons with total control of the ball.

David itched to get in there and dig out the ball. He held his position hoping the forwards would do the job.

"Come on, Myles, get the ball," he yelled.

No such luck. The wall of green sweaters kept on coming. Into the action he went. His foot got a piece of the ball but the Falcons retained possession. Aw, man. He tried again. This time the ball popped out and Rob booted it out of bounds. Green ball.

"Good going, Rob," he called.

David tried to calm himself as he waited for the throw in. The Falcons had been putting the screws to the Hornets for what felt like forever. He knew it could only have been minutes. No matter, one unlucky break and they would have a tie game. These were the play-off rounds now and that would mean settling the game by penalty kicks. It would be game over for the Hornets, then. Sandy had become an okay goalie, but, he just didn't have it in him to stop a one-on-one.

The throw-in bounced off a player on the other team and landed at David's feet.

"Heads up, Patrick," he called.

He passed it to his friend and the play went down the field. David ran after it. Let the whistle blow, he prayed.

"How much time?" he yelled to Kevin standing on the sidelines. The boy only shrugged.

Rats. The Hornets had lost the ball. Here came the Falcons again. David took a deep breath and dove into the thick of things. Try as he might, he couldn't gain possession of the ball. All he could do was slow down the play. The Falcons inched their way towards Sandy.

Then, suddenly the ball was gone. Tiny little Adam had squeezed in among the green and managed to kick the ball out of bounds.

David chuckled. He wants a trophy all right — real bad.

"Mark a green shirt. Don't leave them open," Prescott yelled.

David tagged a Falcon to shadow. The ball was tossed into the air and the ref blew the whistle. Game over.

Exhausted, he flopped on the grass. He sprayed himself with his water bottle, then he took a long cold guzzle.

Patrick dropped down beside David and grabbed his own drink. "Aw, rats. It's empty."

"Here," David passed his bottle to him. " Geez, that was too close. I'm pooped."

Patrick gulped the last few mouthfuls of water. "We almost bit the dust that last play. Oh, well, one game down and two to go."

"I wish they'd have all the play-off games on the same weekend, like in a tournament. This week's going to drag," David said.

"No kidding." Patrick waved as he hopped into his dad's car.

David couldn't concentrate over the next few days. His mind was on soccer. It was a good thing a field trip was planned for Thursday — game day. That would be like no school at all.

* * *

"Look, Mom, I'm fine." David pointed to the 'V' in his collarbone. "See, I'm not sucking in. The medication worked. Please let me play. I've got to. It's the semi-finals."

"David are you crazy? Of course you can't play. Just look at you. You've used your inhaler twice in the last half hour and you're wheezing." His mother raked her hand through her hair.

"I'm fine. Why won't you believe me?"

He ran up the stairs to his bedroom, slamming the door behind him. That was stupid, he thought. The exertion had left him sucking for air.

"It's not fair. It's not fair. It's not fair ..."

David climbed onto his bed. He pulled his knees to his chest and hugged them. Teeth clenched, he let the tears roll down his cheeks and drip off his chin. There was a light tap on his door. He turned his back to it. He didn't want his mother fussing all over him. Not now.

"Go away," he said.

The door opened anyway. He refused to turn around. A gentle hand squeezed his shoulder.

"She's worried for you, son. That's all," Gramps said.

"I don't care. My breathing will be okay. I hate the farm and I hate cottonwoods." David pounded the bed with his fists.

"Cottonwoods? Farms? Boy, you're not making any sense." Gramps sat down on the bed beside him.

David turned to face his grandfather. He wiped his sleeve across his eyes to dry the tears.

"We went on a field trip to a farm today. In the yard, there was this big old cottonwood tree. It was covered with fluff. The ground looked like it had snowed. Fluff was blowing everywhere. I could feel it tickle my face. It went in my nose and mouth. I couldn't stop sneezing. It caused my asthma, I'm sure of it."

"That's too bad, son. And on such an important day, too." Gramps put his arm around David's shoulder.

"Shush. Gramps listen."

They both listened intently.

"I don't hear anything," Gramps whispered.

"Exactly. I've stopped wheezing." He looked at his grandfather. Brown eyes pleading. "Tell Mom I can play."

"Now, son, you know I can't do that. Your mother is right. You shouldn't play this soon after an attack. But maybe we can compromise." Gramps stood up and extended his gnarled fingers. David placed his small hand in the warm palm and let himself be led down into the kitchen.

"Shirley, I've got a proposition for —" Gramps started to say.

David's mom whirled around. She poked Gramps in the chest with her index finger.

"Dad, butt out for once. He can't play and that's that."

"Calm down, girl. I agree with you. He can't play, but maybe he can go watch? It's important to him."

"Forget it. What if he has another attack?"

Forehead creased. Eyes glaring. She tried to stare down Gramps. He returned her stare.

"Will staying home prevent it?"

"Well, no." She broke the eye contact.

"Then, what's the problem?" Gramps pressed on.

"I might have to take him to the hospital."

"You can take him from the field, can't you?"

"I suppose …"

Was she weakening? Gramps took her hand and patted it.

"That's a girl. You'll be there. I'll be there. The hospital is closer to the field than our house. What more could you want? Let's give him a break, okay?"

David's mother pulled her hand out of Gramps' grasp.

"Don't badger me. Give me time to think." She covered her eyes with her hand for a moment. "Okay. We'll go. I hope I don't regret this."

David threw himself at his mom, nearly knocking her over.

"Oh, thank you. Thank you, Mom." He hugged her tightly.

Behind her back, Gramps winked at David.

"I'm going to wear my uniform, even if I can't play." He raced up and changed quickly.

"Come on, let's go." He grabbed their arms and dragged them out to the car.

"I'll get the chairs from the trunk, Dad, you go with David and explain things to the coach," David's mother said as she pulled in to the parking lot.

"Mom, couldn't Gramps get the chairs and you come with me?" He didn't want there to be any more trouble between his grandfather and the coach.

"What's the matter, dear? You've never needed me to hold your hand before. Is it your asthma? Should we go home?"

He decided to nip that bud fast. "Heck, no. I just wanted you to meet the coach."

"Don't be silly, David. You know I've talked to Mr. Prescott many times before. Now, get going."

"Come on, son." Gramps started off across the field. David followed slowly. The coach was gathering the balls used during the warm-up when Gramps reached him.

"Excuse me, Coach Prescott?"

"Yes?" The coach looked up frowning. He quickly changed his expression to a pleasant one.

"Hello, sir, hello. What can I do for you?"

"Well," Gramps started to say, but Prescott had noticed David.

"Please excuse me a minute. You're late, boy. The game's about to start."

Gramps reached out and put his hands on David's shoulder. "I'm afraid he can't play today, coach. He's had an asthma attack. But, we couldn't keep him away from such a big game. Right, David?" Gramps patted him and chuckled.

Coach Prescott's smile widened. "No problem, sir. I'll just cross him off the roster. So this is your …?"

"Grandson."

"It's nice to know which lad our fans are connected to."

The coach was positively beaming. It gave David an un-easy feeling. He gave a little shiver, then turned and walked over to Patrick. He dropped down beside him.

"Hey, boy. You can't stay there." Turning back to Gramps the coach said, "I'm afraid I wouldn't be able to keep an eye on him. I'll be too busy coaching."

"Of course. I'll stay and look after him. Give me a minute. I'll go get my chair." Gramps turned to leave.

"Sorry, sir. That just won't do. I have a policy of not letting the fans sit with the team. Don't want the lads con-fused by others trying to coach them, do we? Can't make exceptions, you understand. My hands are tied. Sorry."

So David followed his grandfather back to the other side of the field. It felt strange sitting with the spectators. He missed the team spirit, the high-fives and pats on the back. His only consolation was Patrick's wave from the field and the Hornets' victory.

David made himself a vow. Nothing was going to stop him from playing the next game — the play-off finals. If there was a chance of anything at school, or anywhere else for that matter, triggering an asthma attack, he was staying home. Playing sick if he had to. Mind, it would have to be something that could be cured quickly. Like a headache.

* * *

David had worried needlessly. The days passed uneventfully.

The evening of the play-off finals, everyone was pumped for the game. The boys were unable to control their excite-ment. It bubbled over in the form of roughhousing. Coach Prescott got frustrated. He made the team sit down, take deep breaths, and count to one hundred. Only then he gave his pep talk and game plan.

As David expected, Patrick sat out the first half with him. They paced the sidelines together like caged lions, their stomachs in tight knots. They had never beaten the Coyotes, but they had tied them once. All the other games had been close.

"I hate games like this," David said.

"No kidding — just back and forth, back and forth in the middle half of the field."

"Yeah, and no breakaways. Nothing to take away the butterflies. Not even for a moment."

By half time it was still a scoreless tie. The Hornets were playing a strong game.

David downed his orange juice. Carefully, he adjusted his shin pads and socks. He closed his eyes and took slow deliberate breaths, preparing himself mentally for his shift on the field. Ready. He waited for Coach Prescott to assign him his position.

"Okay lads, get out on the field. James, that's left field. No, Jocko, left not right. That's it. Sandy, play out a bit. All right. Good. Give it your best shot, lads. Good luck."

David hadn't heard his name called. He looked around. There was only Adam left beside him, doing jumping-jacks. Prescott must have made a mistake. He ran to the coach and tapped him lightly on the arm.

"Coach, sir, I think you missed me. It's my half to play."

Prescott looked at his roster. He had that strange smile on his face — the one he had smiled when he'd told Gramps that he liked to know who the kids belonged to.

"Hum. Ah, yes. You haven't played yet, have you? They're just about to start. I'll have to sub you in at our next whistle."

The whistle came and went. The game resumed. David hadn't been subbed in. He decided to shadow the coach. Maybe that way Prescott would remember him. But the second break in play also resumed without him.

David tapped the coach's arm again.

"Sir, you said —"

"Oh, yeah, yeah. Next whistle." Prescott flicked his wrist as if swatting bugs. He didn't even bother to look up.

David could no longer focus on the game. He wanted his turn so badly. All he could do was watch the ref, hoping to hear the whistle. So, when it blew, he acted immediately.

"Coach, sir, you said you'd sub me in. Two whistles have come and gone. It's my half to play."

"For heaven's sake. Go sit down. I'm trying to concentrate on the game. I don't need you telling me how to coach. I'll sub you in when I sub you in." Prescott spat the words through clenched teeth.

The coach grabbed David roughly by the shoulder. He spun him around and gave him a slight push.

David stumbled, then caught his balance. His face flushed red. He glanced sideways at Myles' and Sandy's dads standing on the sidelines. Had they witnessed his humiliation? But wait, parents aren't supposed to be with the team. Isn't that what the coach had told Gramps?

He dropped down beside Adam. His anger swallowed everything around him. The tape in his head kept on playing: *He's mean. I didn't know he could be so mean. I hate him. I hate him. I hate him.*

Nothing penetrated his rage. When Adam jumped on him, he realized that the Hornets had scored, but it barely registered. Then a light squeeze on his shoulder and soft-spoken words broke his trance.

"David, are you all right, son?"

"Gramps?" David stood up.

"Are you okay? Is your asthma acting up again?"

"No, no. I'm fine. I just want to play," he mumbled.

Gramps gently held David at arm's length. "Then why aren't you on the field? There's only ten minutes left in the game."

"He won't play me. He keeps saying next whistle. But he won't sub me in, Gramps."

"For crying out loud! What's wrong with that man Prescott? Got mush where his brain should be. No concept of fairness. You paid the same money as the rest — you should play the same as the others. I'm going to give him a piece of my mind." Gramps' eyes were flashing. His arms were waving. The words came out in loud explosive bursts.

Prescott heard and came running.

"You're going to play, lad. Not to worry, you're going to play." He threw an arm around David and pulled him to the sidelines. Away from Gramps.

"You said that before."

"I know, lad. I know. Too many things to remember."

"I reminded you. You just pushed me away. The game's almost over now."

"The time just wasn't right to put you in — momentum and all. It was a tough coaching call. But you'll get your chance. Ah, there's our whistle." Prescott waved frantically at the ref. "Subs. Subs."

David was on the field. He watched. A throw-in. A pass. A long boot. Then the whistle blew. He barely had time to adjust, let alone get into the game, before it was over. David stood there stunned.

The team went wild. Sandy walked around shaking hands saying, "Revenge is a dish best served cold." The kids acted as if they understood the wisdom of the *Klingon* saying. Myles did the jock thing. He hugged everyone, even Patrick. And Patrick hugged back.

David went through the motions of accepting congratulations and shaking hands. He felt apart from the team through it all.

As the convener handed him his medal, he heard Prescott say, "Good game, lad."

They were the same words he had said to each of the other boys, but David felt they were a personal insult. A strong urge to kick the coach came over him. He pinned a smile on his face and kicked a clump of dirt instead.

"Slushies all around, on me. And after? Pizza party at my house." Prescott was all smiles.

The formalities over, David fled to his mother's car. No way was he going to that jerk's house.

11

David's Dilemma

Victory. David never thought winning the championship could feel so empty. He stared at the copper shield that lay in the palm of his hand. With his finger, he traced the raised design, laurel wreath and scroll. STBV DIVISIONAL CHAMPIONS was engraved on the scroll. The medal weighed heavy in his hands. It was almost as heavy as his heart.

"Well, let's have a look at it." His mom held out her hand for the medal.

David stopped tracing the design with his finger and handed her the shield.

"Isn't it wonderful! My son, divisional champ." She beamed at him.

"Yeah, right! Straight from the bench." David thumped the kitchen table with his fist.

Gramps reached over and patted David's hand. "One game does not a championship make, son. You earned that medal, fair and square."

"Oh, I know that, Gramps. I played my best every game. I never let the team down. But Prescott never saw that. You know something — even though I'm glad the team won, I'd still rather have played more."

"And that's the way it should be." Gramps smiled at David as he shuffled out.

David waited until he heard his grandfather's door shut.

"Mom, can I ask you something ..." David's mother looked at him expectantly as he hesitated. "Something about Dad?"

"Sweetie, you know you can, anything, anytime. What do you want to know?"

"Do you think Dad would have been proud of me, now that I won a soccer medal?"

"Of course, honey. David, your Dad would have been proud of you if you had drooled all over him. He was so looking forward to your birth."

"But soccer was important to him, right?"

"Well now, how can I put this? Yes, soccer was important to him, but only because it gave him a chance to be with his friends. If his friends had been into square dancing, he'd have been a square dancer. No, maybe not. He wouldn't have looked good in those frilly dresses. He didn't have the legs for it."

"Mom, I'm serious. He really, really liked soccer."

"David, soccer was just the game he grew up playing. It was fun. He certainly wasn't obsessed with it. He didn't follow it on TV. He didn't even watch the World Cup. He liked to play, that's all."

"But what about all those soccer pictures? My memory book is full of soccer pictures. I just thought ..."

"Oh, that. The silly man was camera shy. The only time I could take pictures of him, without him grabbing the camera, was when he wasn't looking. At his games, he was too busy to notice. David, I'm sorry you got the wrong idea. They were the best photos of him that I had, and I wanted you to have the best."

"Oh." This would take some getting used to.

He shook his head. Oh, well, *he* still enjoyed the sport. And anyway, his father had played soccer, hadn't he?

Once in his room, David tossed the medal into his junk drawer. He tore off his soccer uniform and chucked it into a corner of his closet.

Waves of disappointment came over him. He felt betrayed by the Rejects. None of them seemed to have noticed he hadn't been on the field. What were they doing, he wondered? Having a good time, no doubt, scarfing down pizza with Prescott.

There were footsteps on the stairs. His door burst open.

"Davie, my man, why'd you take off so fast? Never mind. Pizza's on the table and I'm starving." Patrick grabbed David's arm and pulled him down the stairs.

Rob and Kevin were sitting in the kitchen.

"I thought you'd be celebrating with the coach." David pulled out a chair and sat down.

"Join the enemy? Are you kidding? After the way he treated you today? No way man!" Patrick tossed David a can of cola.

Kevin lifted his orange pop. "A toast — to the Divisional Champs."

They banged their canned drinks. The pop fizzed, spilling and mixing together on the table.

"Hey, I wonder if that's how *swamp juice* was invented?" Rob dipped a spidery finger into the sticky mess, then licked it.

"Maybe," Patrick said. He lifted his drink again. "Here's to the *City Play-offs*. Rejects rule."

* * *

David was in a daze. The *City's*. He'd forgotten that becoming the Divisional Champs meant going to the City Play-offs.

In all his years of soccer, just getting to the Divisional's had been a hard fought goal. Then last year things had jelled.

They had made it, not only to the play-offs, but all the way to the finals. He vaguely remembered there being talk about going to the *City's*.

Coach Rooda had said, "Let's cross that bridge when we come to it. For now, focus on the job at hand." But they had lost and the season had ended.

This year, David had been consumed with just playing well and showing Prescott that he was worthy of a spot on the team. In the end, it hadn't mattered. He and the rest of the Rejects had stayed as invisible to the coach at the end as on the first day. By the time the last congrats were said after that final game, David had been glad to be done with the season. He had hoped never to cross paths with Prescott again.

But the season wasn't over after all.

David felt pulled in two directions. Just thinking about Prescott made him angry. How could he play in the fall? But then, if he quit, he'd be letting down his teammates. His stomach gave another lurch. David swallowed hard and shook his head. He needed to talk to someone — someone grown up.

David found himself standing in front of Gramps' room. His subconscious had made the decision for him. David knocked on the door.

"What's the matter, son?" Gramps said as he waved him in.

"I need to talk."

"Okay. Here, have a seat," his grandfather patted the bed as he lowered himself into the chair beside it.

David sat on the edge of the bed, legs swinging, trying to find the right words.

"Well …" encouraged Gramps.

"I hate Prescott," David blurted out.

"And …"

"And I don't ever want to play for him again. But I … I have to." He twisted the bottom edge of his T-shirt in his hands.

"Why ever for? If he coaches next year, we transferred to another community club. Don't worry." The old man reached over and grasped David's hand in his gnarled ones.

"But, you don't understand. We won the Divisonal's. The season isn't over. We're in the City Play-offs in September. He's still my coach."

"You don't have to play for him any more, if you don't want to. After what happened, no one would blame you for quitting."

"I know, but I'd be letting the team down and I don't want to do that either."

"You do have a man-sized dilemma then, don't you? So ... what are you going to do?"

"I don't know. You tell me, Gramps."

"I can't do that, son. You wouldn't be satisfied unless you made the decision yourself. My advice to you is to make lists of all the reasons for staying with the team and all the reasons for quitting. Then decide what to do, okay?"

David nodded.

"So, off you go. Good luck."

David ran up the stairs two at a time. He grabbed the blue binder off his desk and tore out a sheet of loose-leaf. He stared at the blank sheet for a moment. Carefully, using a ruler, he drew a line down the middle of the page. On one side of it he wrote 'Reasons to Stay' and on the other, 'Reasons to Quit'. He started to fill in the first column. It surprised him how fast and easy the words came.

1) I don't want to let down the team.

2) I have fun when I play.

3) I'd really, REALLY like to play in a city play-offs.

4) I play hard so I belong on the team.

5) I like being with the guys.

6) I love soccer.

He moved on to the next column. In big letters he wrote —
1) I HATE PRESCOTT!

His mind went blank so he retraced the words until they were big and black. He could think of no other reason. But wasn't that reason enough? Those three words seemed to hold more weight than all the words on the other side. This wasn't helping at all. He decided to go talk to Gramps again.

David found his grandfather in the living room. "Gramps, I still can't figure it out."

The old man lowered the paper he was reading. He looked over his glasses at his grandson. "Hum … what's that?"

"I said my lists didn't help."

"Here." Gramps reached for the loose-leaf sheet. "What's the problem? As I see it, one list is definitely longer than the other."

"But, Gramps, some feelings are stronger than others."

"How right you are. Feelings sure can get in the way of logic, can't they? Tell me something. If it wasn't for Prescott, would you stick with the team?"

"Are you kidding? That's a no-brainer."

"So, you're going to let that jerk control you?"

"He's not controlling me, Gramps."

"Sure he is. You're not going to play because of him. And playing is something you really want to do, see?"

"Oh Gramps, I can't face him. I'd be too embarrassed."

"What have you got to be ashamed about?" His grandfather stared him straight in the eyes.

"Nothing. It's just … he was such a creep that last game. And when he yelled at me everyone heard."

"So what? He's the one who should be mortified. Someone needs to teach that man a thing or two about respect and fair play. Imagine humiliating a child just because he asked for his rightful turn on the field!"

For a moment, his grandfather sat there silently.

"Have you ever been bullied, David?" he asked.

"Yeah, Myles likes to push his weight around sometimes. No big deal. He does it to everyone. If you ignore him or hold your ground he'll leave you alone. Most bullies do."

"And when you do that, how do you feel?"

"Pretty good, I guess. But what's that got to do with Prescott? Oh, I get it ... he's a bully. Just bigger and older than the ones I'm used to."

"Plain and simple. Look at it that way and deal with it accordingly."

"I guess I'll stay then."

"There's no guess about it, David. Hold your head high. Do what you know is right for you."

David squared his shoulders and tilted his chin a little.

"Yeah. I'm playing. I'm going to the *City's* and no jerk is going to stop me," he said.

12

Rejects' Revenge

"Well, Shirley, ready for some fireworks? Go get your car keys, girl." Gramps had on his cap. His light beige summer jacket was draped over his arm.

"Dad, what in heaven's name are you talking about?" David's mom looked up from the papers she was organizing. They were spread out before her on the kitchen table.

"Prescott. The community club's board is meeting tonight."

The coach's name caught David's attention. His hand drifted away from the pop he was reaching for and clamped on to the carton of skimmed milk. They wouldn't send him from the room if he was fixing himself a mug of hot chocolate. Mom was always bugging him to drink more of that yucky white stuff.

"You're still not making any sense. I have no idea what the board meeting has to do with you or me." His mom kept shuffling her papers.

"We're making a presentation about Prescott to the board tonight. At least I am. You can just watch if you like. I set it all up, just like we agreed."

"When you spoke to me last Friday, I thought you meant you were going to write them a letter."

"Heck no. Wouldn't want to do that. They would just table the letter, set it aside and deal with it after the season. Then they'd send a nice little note saying, 'Thanks for your information. We acted upon your concerns and everything's okey-dokey now.' Nope, it's best to be present, so they have to deal with the problem then and there."

David could no longer contain himself.

"But Gramps, you said no one could do anything about the coach," he blurted out.

"That's not quite what I said. If I remember correctly, I said there was nothing you kids could do. Now an adult — that's a different story."

"Why now? Why didn't you do something earlier?"

"I figured the season was almost over. Didn't think he could do any more damage."

"Boy, were you wrong. He turned out to be a bigger low-life than you gave him credit for," Mom said.

"Time's a-wasting. Let's get going."

"Dad, I wish you had consulted with me before setting this up."

"But, I thought I did. You said you supported me."

"I do. I want to be there but I can't tonight. I have a meeting of my own." She carefully gathered up her papers and put them into a folder.

"Sorry, Shirley. Wasn't thinking once again. Don't fret, I'll do a good job."

"I'm sure you will. That's not what I'm worried about. It's David."

David snapped his head in his mom's direction. "What about me?"

"There's no one to look after you if we are both out tonight. My meeting is job related. Dad, you'll just have to cancel — "

"Mom, no. I want Prescott to get what's coming to him," David interrupted.

"I do too, dear. But tonight's impossible. Maybe we can reschedule for the next meeting of the board."

"That's not until September. By then, it will be too late."

"Mom, I can go with Gramps to the clubhouse. There's always something going on there. I'll sit by the gym." David wasn't going to let his chance for justice slip through his fingers.

"You know, Shirley, maybe he *should* come to the meeting. Might do some good, hearing things from the horse's mouth." The old man rubbed his chin.

"Don't be silly. It's a school night. Meetings always go late."

"But, Mom, you're forgetting — tomorrow is an inservice day — no school. Pleease?"

"Shirley, I'll ask them to put me first on the agenda. I'll get him home at a decent hour. It's now or never."

"Oh, all right. I'm trusting you, Dad." She waved and left.

"Gramps, can Patrick come too?"

"I don't know, son."

"He can explain things better than I can. He's got more guts. Please," David interrupted.

"It's okay with me, but it's up to his mom. And I'm making the call. I won't have you boys plotting anything."

"ALL RIGHT."

* * *

Patrick climbed into the back seat of Gramps' car. "Is it true Mr. Gates that you're going to the meeting to kick Prescott's butt? And we're going to tell our side?"

"Well, let's put it this way — we're going to tell the truth. We'll let the board handle the discipline, shall we?"

On the way there, the boys discussed what they were going to say.

"We have to tell about how unfair he was to you that last game."

David nodded. "And how some kids played all the time."

"And how he didn't coach us."

"And —"

"Okay, boys, we're here." Gramps pulled into the parking lot. They followed him silently as he wound his way to the boardroom. He strode right in. The boys hesitated before entering, intimidated by the formal space. The windowless room was paneled in dark wood. In the center, there was a long table surrounded by chairs. There were twelve people sitting there, nine men and three women. One of the women sat at the head of the table. She was holding a small wooden mallet. For a moment, David was mesmerized by her long, blood red fingernails. He didn't know who she was. For that matter, he didn't recognize many of them — just a couple of his classmates' dads and Prescott. Mr. Rooda was there, also. He and the coach were sitting together.

"Ah, Mr. Gates. I'm Jan Budzilka. You're early. We had you scheduled at the end of the meeting," said the lady at the head of the table.

"I was hoping you could put me on first. You see I've brought the boys, seeing that it involves them. And I'd like to get them home at a decent hour."

Coach Rooda pushed back his chair and came to the door. "I'm not comfortable with the boys being here. The discussions can get quite heated."

"I agree. Children exaggerate. I'm sure Mr. Gates can explain their concerns more objectively," Sandy's dad said.

A number of the board members nodded in agreement.

Gramps shrugged his shoulders. "If you think that's for the best, Mr. Rooda. I had planned on presenting the case by myself originally."

Rats, David thought.

"Why don't you boys go to the gym. There's a drop-in taking place right now," their former coach suggested.

Gramps patted David's shoulder. "Off you go."

As they walked down the hall, they heard Mr. Rooda say to Gramps, "It can get quite stuffy in here, so we need to leave the door open."

Halfway down the hall, David grabbed Patrick. "I *wanted* to be there."

"Come on. Let's go back then." His friend spun around.

"Patrick, you're crazy. You heard what they said. They're not going to let us in. They won't listen to kids. Gramps will do the job."

"Who said anything about going into the room. Don't you want to know what they're saying? It won't be our fault if we hear them talking. *They* left the door open." Patrick grinned and raised his eyebrows up and down.

"Let's do it."

They tiptoed back, keeping close to the wall. By the door, they slid down it to a sitting position. They could hear the adults' voices loud and clear.

David nudged Patrick. "Look at that sign," he whispered into his friend's ear.

The interior of the boardroom was reflected in the glass covering the large poster.

Gramps had seated himself opposite Prescott.

"... Mr. McDonald and I'm Bill Rooda, Soccer Convener for the club. Mr. Prescott you already know. I hope you don't mind that I asked him to join us," their last year's coach finished the introductions and sat down.

Gramps acknowledged him with a nod. "Not at all. He needs to hear what I have to say."

For a moment, no one said anything.

"You have the floor, Mr. Gates," said Jan Budzilka.

Gramps pulled out a folded piece of paper and his glasses from his shirt pocket. He unfolded the sheet slowly. He donned his spectacles and cleared his throat.

"Ladies and gentlemen, I've had the opportunity to read your club's mission statement, and a good one it is at that. If you are as child-centered as it implies, then you will understand my concerns. My grandson loves soccer and yet he is dreading the city play-offs. He has even considered quitting —"

"Excuse me, are we talking about David DeMarco?" Coach Rooda interrupted. Gramps nodded. Mr. Rooda shook his head. "That's not like him at all. David's not the type to quit. Why does he want to quit?"

"I'd have to say Mr. Prescott's coaching methods."

David elbowed Patrick's side. "Way to go Gramps," he mouthed.

"I'm sure you'd be the only one who'd question my methods. When I first signed on, this community club didn't have a single soccer trophy. Now go look in the memento cabinet."

"Here, here." A number of the men present rapped on the table. Among them was Sandy's dad.

David rolled his eyes. Good grief. It's only one trophy.

"Winning isn't everything," his grandfather replied.

"Eleven-year-old boys like to win," Coach Prescott said.

"Only if they're playing. Sitting on the sidelines watching doesn't count," Gramps replied.

"I played all the lads."

"Yes, you did, I'll grant you that. But not equally. Some boys played the whole game every time, and others, like my grandson —"

"Oh, come on people. Can't you see what's happening here? I'm being attacked over another case of 'visions of grandeur' — a lad thinks he's the next soccer sensation so he clamours for more field time," Prescott interrupted.

"What a liar. It's not true," David whispered to Patrick.

"Shush," his friend warned.

"Hold on there, Colin. If it were some other kid, I'd say maybe. But DeMarco ..." Bill Rooda shook his head. "I've coached him, he's happy with whatever field time he gets. Let's hear his grandfather out."

Thank you, Coach Rooda, David thought.

"Now, as I was saying, my grandson's group did most of the sitting out. Even at practices, the coach gave them very little attention."

"Look, I did what I had to do. That first day, I knew we could win it all. But it would require intense work. The potential was there. I set the weaker group to do skill-building drills and focused on the stronger ones. Sacrifices are sometimes required when playing on teams. Bill understands that. I'll bet the lads do, too. Just being on a winning team is enough."

"Bull. This discrimination not only made David's group feel inferior, but not part of the team at all."

"You tell 'em, Mr. Gates," Patrick whispered.

"What rubbish!" Coach Prescott rolled his eyes.

"Is that so? Then why do the boys call themselves the Rejects?" Gramps' fist tapped the table lightly for emphasis.

Someone gasped. All eyes turned on the coach.

Prescott's face reddened. "This is news to me. I'm sure Mr. Gates must be mistaken. If the kids were unhappy, all the parents had to do was speak to me."

"I thought I did," Gramps said.

"Look," Mr. Prescott glanced around the table. " If you don't like what I'm doing, I'll be happy to step down. And you can find yourself another coach."

All right! The boys silently high-fived.

"Now you know that's not what we want," Mr. Rooda reached out and patted the coach's shoulder.

"Darn right. Coach Prescott's been wonderful for my boy. You stick to your guns, coach, and we'll stick by you," Sandy's dad added.

Patrick stuck his tongue out.

"Nonetheless, we can't have our children thinking of themselves as rejects. Our club's policy is to include all kids," Mrs. Budzilka reminded them.

"No problem. Have two teams. That way the outstanding lads will have a chance to play at a level they deserve," suggested Prescott.

"Look, Colin, I know where you're coming from. You've almost always played at an elite level of soccer. But our club is a small one. There just aren't enough kids in the area to do that. In any case, there aren't any superstars here. We prefer to emphasize fitness and enjoyment of sport."

"Besides, to stay afloat, we need every dollar we get from our members. We can't afford to have players quit. So far, focusing on the fun has worked for our club," added the president.

"Well … you know what's best for your club. I'll do it your way. But I won't guarantee results." Colin Prescott shrugged his shoulders and threw his hands in the air.

Patrick wrinkled his nose. "Rats," he mouthed.

Yeah. Double rats. They were stuck with the creep. David sighed.

"Well, Mr. Gates, does this satisfy your concerns?"

"Not quite. There's one other thing I'd like to add. I think my grandson is due an apology from Coach Prescott. In the final match, he made David sit out almost the entire game."

David's heart swelled with affection.

"Excuse me, but isn't this a bit extreme? It's not like I did it intentionally."

LIAR. Liar, you did too. I reminded you, you jerk, David thought.

"You know how it is, Bill. You're in the heat of the game. The momentum is great. You're concentrating on coaching.

So something slipped my mind. I'm only human," Prescott continued.

Gramps, say something, David prayed.

But his grandfather sat back quietly. Just when the silence was becoming uncomfortable, he cleared his throat.

"Mr. Prescott, I owe you an apology," he said.

Patrick's jaw dropped.

"You're right. There's only one of you. What you need is a team manager. You know, someone to do the joe jobs. Jobs like putting the equipment away after warm ups, filling out the game sheet, subbing in the lines. That way you could concentrate on the coaching."

Angry tears stung David's eyes.

"Exactly. Unfortunately, they're hard to come by." The coach was nodding eagerly.

"Just to show you there's no hard feelings, I offer my services."

"Um ... er ... well now, I appreciate your offer. But you really don't know the game."

"Hey. I said I'd only do the easy stuff. How hard could subbing lines be? Just like doing a tune up on a car. I replace spark plugs with spark plugs and rotors with rotors, if you know what I mean. Of course, you'd decide the positions."

David relaxed. Patrick smiled.

"I don't know ..."

"Look, I can see you have your doubts. Mr. Rooda, is your team playing in the fall?" Gramps turned to the convener.

Mr. Rooda shook his head.

"How about giving me a hand the first few weeks? That way I won't be a burden on the coach. I'd be mighty grateful. What do you say?"

"Yeah ... I suppose I could do that. I intended to cheer the team on anyway."

"It's all set then. Right, Coach?" Gramps extended his hand across the table to Mr. Prescott.

The coach hesitated. He looked around the table for help, but he found none. He took the old man's hand reluctantly.

Patrick could no longer contain himself. A guffaw escaped his lips.

In the room, all heads turned towards the door.

David didn't wait to be discovered. He jumped up and ran straight down the hall and right out of the building. Patrick was close on his heels. The boys collapsed on the grass, trying to control the laughter.

"This ... is ... just too sweet," Patrick gasped.

"Gramps is awesome." David started to giggle again.

The laughter subsided.

"Oh, man," his friend sighed.

"Trust Gramps to be sneaky. Do you realize what he did? In one move he got himself *and* Coach Rooda on the team. A few weeks — that's the whole play-offs. They'll be watching Prescott. He'll have to treat us fairly with the convener there. And Gramps will make sure we're all played equally — he'll be doing the subbing. Slick, huh?"

"Old Prescott never saw it coming." Patrick's husky body shook with renewed laughter.

"To tell you the truth, I never saw it coming, either. For a moment there I actually thought my grandfather had given up."

"I wish the play-offs were now. I wish we didn't have to wait until September to see the screws put to Prescott." Patrick wiped tears from his eyes.

Much as David would have liked to see the coach squirm, he had had enough conflict to last a lifetime. The holidays would give Prescott time to get used to the idea he was stuck with Gramps and stuck with the Rejects. And it would give time a chance to soften his hatred for the man.

"Maybe it's better this way, with the summer in between. It'll be like starting fresh. A new team," David said.

The door to the clubhouse banged open. Prescott stormed by, mumbling. "No vision at all. Satisfied with mediocrity. The Rejects — hrump." He slammed his car door and squealed out of the parking lot.

The boys burst out laughing again.

"REJECTS, REVENGE!" David raised a fist into the air.

"Hoowee. How sweet it is." Patrick raised an arm, too.

SMACK! The boys' palms slapped a triumphant high-five.

Other books you'll enjoy in the Sports Stories series ...

Baseball

☐ *Curve Ball* by John Danakas #1
Tom Poulos is looking forward to a summer of baseball in Toronto until his mother puts him on a plane to Winnipeg.

☐ *Baseball Crazy* by Martyn Godfrey #10
Rob Carter wins an all-expenses-paid chance to be batboy at the Blue Jays spring training camp in Florida.

☐ *Shark Attack* by Judi Peers #25
The East City Sharks have a good chance of winning the county championship until their arch rivals get a tough new pitcher.

☐ *Hit and Run* by Dawn Hunter and Karen Hunter #35
Glen Thomson is a talented pitcher, but as his ego inflates, team morale plummets. Will he learn from being benched for losing his temper?

Basketball

☐ *Fast Break* by Michael Coldwell #8
Moving from Toronto to small-town Nova Scotia was rough, but when Jeff makes the school basketball team he thinks things are looking up.

☐ *Camp All-Star* by Michael Coldwell #12
In this insider's view of a basketball camp, Jeff Lang encounters some unexpected challenges.

☐ *Nothing but Net* by Michael Coldwell #18
The Cape Breton Grizzly Bears prepare for an out-of-town basketball tournament they're sure to lose.

☐ *Slam Dunk* by Steven Barwin and Gabriel David Tick #23
In this sequel to *Roller Hockey Blues*, Mason Ashbury's basketball team adjusts to the arrival of some new players: girls.

☐ *Courage on the Line* by Cynthia Bates #33
After Amelie changes schools, she must confront difficult former teammates in an extramural match.

☐ *Free Throw* by Jacqueline Guest #35
Matthew Eagletail must adjust to a new school, a new team and a new father along with five pesky sisters.

☐ *Triple Threat* by Jacqueline Guest #38
Matthew's cyber-pal Free Throw comes to visit, and together they face a bully on the court.

☐ *Queen of the Court* by Michele Martin Bossley #40
What happens when the school's fashion queen winds up on the basketball court?

Figure Skating

☐ *A Stroke of Luck* by Kathryn Ellis #6
Strange accidents are stalking one of the skaters at the Millwood Arena.

☐ *The Winning Edge* by Michele Martin Bossley #28
Jennie wants more than anything to win a gruelling series of competitions, but is success worth losing her friends?

☐ *Leap of Faith* by Michele Martin Bossley #36
Amy wants to win at any cost, until a injury makes skating almost impossible. Will she go on?

Gymnastics

☐ *The Perfect Gymnast* by Michele Martin Bossley #9
Abby's new friend has all the confidence she needs, but she also has a serious problem that nobody but Abby seems to know about.

Ice Hockey

☐ *Two Minutes for Roughing* by Joseph Romain #2
As a new player on a tough Toronto hockey team, Les must fight to fit in.

☐ *Hockey Night in Transcona* by John Danakas #7
Cody Powell gets promoted to the Transcona Sharks first line, bumping out the coach's son who's not happy with the change.

☐ *Face Off* by C.A. Forsyth #13
A talented hockey player finds himself competing with his best friend for a spot on a select team.

☐ *Hat Trick* by Jacqueline Guest #20
The only girl on an all-boys' hockey team works to earn the captain's respect and her mother's approval.

☐ *Hockey Heroes* by John Danakas #22
A left-winger on the thirteen-year-old Transcona Sharks adjusts to a new best friend and his mom's boyfriend.

☐ *Hockey Heat Wave* by C.A. Forsyth #27
In this sequel to *Face Off*, Zack and Mitch encounter some trouble when it looks like only one of them will make the select team at hockey camp.

☐ *Shoot to Score* by Sandra Richmond #31
Playing defence on the B list alongside the coach's mean-spirited son is a tough obstacle for Steven to overcome, but he perseveres and changes his luck.

Riding

☐ *A Way With Horses* by Peter McPhee #11
A young Alberta rider invited to study show jumping at a posh local riding school uncovers a secret.

☐ *Riding Scared* by Marion Crook #15
A reluctant new rider struggles to overcome her fear of horses.

☐ *Katie's Midnight Ride* by C.A. Forsyth #16
An ambitious barrel racer finds herself without a horse weeks before her biggest rodeo.

☐ *Glory Ride* by Tamara L. Williams #21
Chloe Anderson fights memories of a tragic fall for a place on the Ontario Young Riders' Team.

☐ *Cutting it Close* by Marion Crook #24
In this novel about barrel racing, a talented young rider finds her horse is in trouble just as she is about to compete in an important event.

☐ *Shadow Ride* by Tamara L. Williams #37
Bronwen has to choose between competing aggressively for herself or helping out a teammate.

Roller Hockey
☐ *Roller Hockey Blues* by Steven Barwin and Gabriel David Tick #17
Mason Ashbury faces a summer of boredom until he makes the roller-hockey team.

Running
☐ *Fast Finish* by Bill Swan #30
Noah is a promising young runner headed for the provincial finals when he suddenly decides to withdraw from the event.

Sailing
☐ *Sink or Swim* by William Pasnak #5
Dario can barely manage the dog paddle, but thanks to his mother he's spending the summer at a water sports camp.

Soccer
☐ *Lizzie's Soccer Showdown* by John Danakas #3
When Lizzie asks why the boys and girls can't play together, she finds herself the new captain of the soccer team.

☐ *Alecia's Challenge* by Sandra Diersch #32
Thirteen-year-old Alecia has to cope with a new school, a new stepfather and friends who have suddenly discovered the opposite sex.

☐ *Shut-Out!* by Camilla Reghelini Rivers #39
David wants to play soccer more than anything, but will the new coach let him?

Swimming

☐ *Water Fight!* by Michele Martin Bossley #14
Josie's perfect sister is driving her crazy but when she takes up swimming — Josie's sport — it's too much to take.

☐ *Taking a Dive* by Michele Martin Bossley #19
Josie holds the provincial record for the butterfly, but in this sequel to *Water Fight,* she can't seem to match her own time and might not go on to the nationals.

☐ *Great Lengths* by Sandra Diersch #26
Fourteen-year-old Jessie decides to find out whether the rumours about a new swimmer at her Vancouver club are true.

Track and Field

☐ *Mikayla's Victory* by Cynthia Bates #29
Mikayla must compete against her friend if she wants to represent her school at an important track event.